THE CHICANERY OF PACO IBAÑEZ

When Marshal Thornton Wilde takes delivery of two prisoners, one of them is the son he hasn't seen for twenty years! Then, there is a jailbreak with Thornton and the town drunk in hot pursuit. Gradually a complicated plot unfolds involving a series of bank robberies and a Mexican peasant with lofty ambitions. Somebody is desperate to keep Wilde and the Texas Rangers away from El Paso, but it's there the amazing truth is revealed and justice meted out.

Books by Jack Sheriff
in the Linford Western Library:

BURY HIM DEEP, IN TOMBSTONE
THE MAN FROM THE STAKED PLAINS
INCIDENT AT POWDER RIVER
BLACK DAY AT HANGDOG
KID KANTRELL
STARLIGHT
BILLY SUNDOWN
THE KILLING AT CIRCLE C
THE LAST WATERHOLE

JACK SHERIFF

THE CHICANERY OF PACO IBAÑEZ

Complete and Unabridged

LINFORD
Leicester

First published in Great Britain in 2008 by
Robert Hale Limited
London

First Linford Edition
published 2009
by arrangement with
Robert Hale Limited
London

The moral right of the author has been asserted

British Library CIP Data

Sheriff, Jack, *1936* –
The chicanery of Paco Ibañez. - -
(Linford western library)
1. Western stories.
2. Large type books.
I. Title II. Series
823.9′14–dc22

ISBN 978–1–84782–928–3

Published by
F. A. Thorpe (Publishing)
Anstey, Leicestershire

Set by Words & Graphics Ltd.
Anstey, Leicestershire
Printed and bound in Great Britain by
T. J. International Ltd., Padstow, Cornwall

This book is printed on acid-free paper

1

October, 1876

The scorching Texas day began with a minor irritation that sent Thornton Wilde crawling around the office on his hands and knees, and managed to get his hackles up as frustration turned to disbelief. It also embarrassed the hell out of him when he realized the town drunk was watching him through the open door as if the performance, coming from the ageing town marshal of Cedar Creek, was nothing out of the ordinary.

By sundown that same day the morning's minor irritation and the incidents that followed in swift succession were finally exposed as terrible portents Wilde had utterly failed to heed. But that morning, unaware that his familiar world was about to be blown apart like a house of cards in a twister, Wilde's main concern was working out how a tin badge he'd dropped while trying to pin it to his vest could disappear off the face of the earth.

He heard the dull clink as it hit the boards. Stood still. Took off the wire-framed glasses he'd been using to read the latest edition of the *Cedar Creek Sentinel*, and let his eyes roam.

The office on the street side of the jail was furnished with iron stove, roll-top desk, one ripped swivel chair and three straight ones for guests — Wilde grinned absently at that — a table under the window, gun rack against the wall and a heck of a lot of dust.

But no badge.

Wilde sighed. He got down on his hands and knees and crawled under the desk, managed to bang his head wriggling out backwards when his broad shoulders got jammed, turned towards the sunlight flooding through the open door with some strange notion of crawling all the way round the office to save climbing to his feet — and saw Gord Bogan.

Wilde had always figured Gord to be either an old thirty or a young fifty. A tall, stringy man with Indian blood in his veins who dressed in rags that looked like clothes, he had appeared out of nowhere some six months ago, and become a familiar sight on the plank walks of the town. He talked mostly common sense, though not a lot of it, and didn't so much walk as wallow: Gord Bogan was a schooner adrift in a current of alcohol that bore him on a sideways tack to places he frequently didn't recognize.

At that moment, Marshal Thornton Wilde was hoping Bogan would drift to join his pesky lost badge — wherever the hell that might be.

'Caught on your pants,' Gord said from the doorway.

Wilde's knee cracked as he stood up.

He twisted backwards, looked where

Gord was pointing, and saw his pants had located what he couldn't: the badge's pin had caught on his left cuff and he'd been taking it with him as he crawled.

'Thanks, Gord,' he said gruffly.

'Strangers in town.'

'Ain't there always?' Wilde said, busy pinning the badge in its rightful position.

'Yeah, but these're trouble.'

Wilde looked up. Bogan was swaying, but his unusual blue eyes were as clear as cool draughts of water, and swirling deep in their depths Wilde saw what could have been concern.

'I'll handle it, Gord,' he said. 'But thanks anyway.'

Somehow, the morning had already been soured.

Wilde watched Bogan wander off down the plank walk in the direction of the Painted Woman saloon, then, finished with the badge, planted his hat on his thinning grey hair and stepped out into the sunshine.

The street was already bustling with life. Women were laughing and talking outside the general store or hurrying up and down the plank walks. Barney Reid was washing the big wooden rifle that hung on chains outside his gunsmith's shop. Across from the Painted Woman, bales of hay were being hoisted from a wagon to the loft over the livery barn. The men doing the hard work were stripped to the waist, the skinny, toothless character directing operations was Denny Wakelin, the man who'd been Cedar Creek's hostler for more than forty years.

Twenty years longer than I've been marshal, Thornton Wilde reflected, and the sobering thought turned his gaze in the opposite direction and he looked up the hill to Jim Lawn's barber shop and, above it, the offices occupied by the Cedar Creek town council.

The direction of Thornton's gaze took his eyes across the limp banner outside the jail reading KEEP AN OLD MAN IN WORK, VOTE THORN

WILDE and, as if drawn by fate he found himself looking at the short, fat figure of Oliver Shank, the man desperate to do the opposite. Shank was the leader of the town council. He wanted Thornton Wilde to retire so he could replace him with his own man. Trouble was, Thornton kept getting voted back in by the citizens of Cedar Creek — and there was not a damn thing Shank could do about it.

Shank, dressed in a shiny black suit, was teetering on the edge of the far plank walk as he talked animatedly to a rawboned character mounted on a rangy grey gelding. The man was half turned in the saddle with most of his weight taken on the right stirrup like someone who's bone weary and saddle sore after riding too far for too long. With his upper body twisted in that manner, Wilde could see the glint of a badge pinned to his vest. That drove his gaze with considerable interest to the two bored men behind the lawman. They were sitting astride wrung-out, trail-stained ponies. From their general demeanour Wilde instantly pegged them as gunslingers. But these were gunslingers who'd reached the end of the trail: their wrists were lashed to the saddle horns, and all three animals were linked by a slack rope.

There's the trouble Gord Bogan was talking about, Wilde thought, unwelcome strife that's come to my town on a day that's begun with a minor irritation and looks like getting worse. And he took a couple of steps to the side, set his back against the warm timber of the jail's wall and leaned back to await developments.

Shank had just about wrapped up the talking, and some kind of decision had been reached. The gaunt lawman seemed to ask a question, and jerked a thumb over his shoulder. As he did so, both prisoners turned and looked directly towards the jail. Shank flapped a hand at the lawman, then turned and strode into the council offices. The lawman touched his horse, wheeled it away from the plank walk. The rope linking the horses snapped tight, and Thornton Wilde thought he heard one of the prisoners utter a gruff protest. Then all three men came down the hill, cut across the street and drew rein at the jail's hitch rail.

The two prisoners glanced at Thornton Wilde. The older of the two spat into the dust. Both men turned away, their manner expressing contempt.

The lawman who'd brought them into town noticed the byplay. He grinned, the humour falling well short of his eyes. He swung out of the saddle, stepped wearily up onto the boards, stripped off a glove and stuck out his hand.

'I'm Reb Tindale, Marshal of San Angelo. You're Thornton Wilde?'

'Right. And you're a long way from home,' Wilde said, moving away from the wall to grasp the other man's hard hand.

'Closer now than yesterday. By tomorrow night I'll be almost there. I caught up with these two in El Paso, in time to prevent them from stepping over the border into Ciudad Juárez. Their saddle-bags were stuffed with cash. If they'd made it into Mexico, a lot of Texas cattlemen would have gone to the wall.'

'They robbed the bank.'

'That's right. Four of them. One of them a Mex. Gunned down the head cashier, left him bleeding to death on the floor of the bank while they forced a young woman to open the safe. They were joined by another man, probably a lookout, when they rode out.'

Wilde frowned. 'Making five in all?'

'Five rode out of San Angelo. Damn near rode my horse to death keepin' up with these two, never saw hide nor hair of the others on the trail. My guess is they were hired guns who hightailed as soon as they got their measly share of the loot. Maybe rode south to cross the border at Del Rio.'

'But you weren't to know that when you set out. One man chasing five doesn't make sense. Why no posse?'

'Would have taken too long to muster the right men, swear them in.' Tindale grinned. 'I figured I could handle it, anyway, and that's the way it worked out.' He raised an eyebrow. 'What about you? I don't see any sign of a deputy. You running a one-man operation?'

Wilde grunted. 'Broke his leg. That's put him out for a week or so, then he'll be hobbling around in plaster and about as much use as a wooden Indian.'

A horse whickered softly and Wilde looked down at the marshal's lean grey mount, the bulging saddle-bags; shifted his gaze and saw the two men watching, listening intently to every work spoken.

'You carryin' that cash with you, Tindale?' Then he grimaced. 'Stupid question; of course you are.'

Tindale nodded. The grin had faded again, and Wilde took note of the clothes stained by hard riding, the lines of strain around the man's eyes, and the way he had turned his back on the prisoners as if they were no longer his responsibility. And he thought again of

Gord Bogan's suggestion that these men were trouble, and wondered for perhaps the first time if that prediction included the marshal, and what form that trouble would take.

'Let me guess,' he said, as Tindale tucked his gloves into his gunbelt and fumbled for the makings. 'You want me to look after the cash and these banditos while you freshen up and get the horses fed and watered — '

'No,' Tindale cut in, shaking his head. 'The cash stays with me, and I'm hitting the trail as soon as I've had a bite to eat — but this time I ride alone. You keep these two here, lock 'em up and hold them.'

'I do? Now why should I do that?'

'It's all been arranged with that cocky fellow in the black suit — what's his name, Shank, your town council supremo? He's agreed you lock up these two hellions, get in touch with the circuit judge. The judge will look at his schedule, set a date for the trial. When that's fixed, let me know.'

'And you'll ride all the way back here to give evidence?' Wilde shook his head. 'Doesn't make sense. The bank robbery was a hundred and fifty miles away in San Angelo. This is a small town on the Pecos river, the nearest telegraph's fifty miles north. You've brought your prisoners this far, without trouble — '

'Yeah, thanks to some luck, but mostly my never ending vigilance. I've watched them through the hours of daylight, cat-napped through each and every night fully expectin' to be jumped at any moment. I'm plumb worn out. The way I feel, I can't guarantee getting them across that river, never mind all the way to San Angelo. Hell, I don't like leaving them here, but the way I see it I've got no choice.'

Wilde hesitated, thought for a long moment then pulled a face.

'Well, I confess I don't like being roped in, but I can understand *and* sympathize.' He sighed. 'OK, let's get them inside.'

He followed Tindale down off the

plank walk and stood to one side with his hand close to his pistol as the marshal drew a pocket knife and set about freeing the two prisoners. Closer now, Wilde looked at them keenly. One was a man in his fifties, dark hair worn long and already turning grey. His frame was as wiry as that of a racing hound. That man grimaced and rubbed his wrists as Tindale slashed through the rawhide bonds, then glanced across at his companion, his colourless eyes blank.

The other man was younger; in his twenties, Wilde estimated — and there was something familiar about him. He was darker than his companion, with a powerful chest and broad shoulders, and in his intelligent blue eyes an unquenchable fire burned. *Not fazed by what's happening*, Wilde judged. *Accepting what comes his way, but always looking for opportunities to swing the situation in his favour. Like me, when I was much younger. Well, there's just a few seconds remaining before he enters my jail, so if he's planning a move he'd better make it fast.*

When the younger man was free and out of the saddle, Wilde glanced at Tindale. No signal passed between them, but Wilde waited until the other lawman had drawn his pistol and positioned himself between the prisoners and the street, then led the way into the jail.

Aware of the scrape and thud of boots behind him, he went straight to the peg-board holding the keys to the cells and took down the heavy ring. Without glancing back he opened the door and strode through to the cell block. There were four cells, all empty. He turned keys in two locks, swung open the heavy doors.

Less than a minute later, the two prisoners were behind bars, the two lawmen back in the office.

'I swear to God,' Tindale said, standing with fists on hips, 'getting that pair off my hands is one hell of a relief.'

'Well, you can now be damn sure the bank's money's safe and those bandits aren't going anywhere in a hurry,' Wilde said.

He flipped his hat onto a peg, sat down behind his desk and reached for pen and paper.

'The official paperwork can wait until later. For now, just give me their names.'

'The older, skinnier man's Gus Allman. The tough-looking youngster's told me nothing except he goes by the moniker of the Waco Kid.'

'And they're wanted for bank robbery?'

'Right.'

'You're a witness?'

'You could say that.'

'What the hell does that mean?'

Tindale grinned. The strain had washed off him. There was even a difference in his posture, Wilde noted. The San Angelo marshal was standing tall, weariness had been replaced by energy and purpose, and his whole demeanour suggested that here was a man keen to get on with unfinished business.

The trouble he's been toting for the past few days has been shifted to another man's shoulders, Wilde thought. But that's not all of it. There's something else, something I'm not seeing. He knew that instinct honed by years of experience as a lawman, was telling him that something was badly wrong — but nothing he had seen or heard appeared to justify those suspicions.

Shaking his head, he pushed away the pen and paper with a grunt that expressed his frustration and uncertainty, but if he'd expected Tindale to take note of his dissatisfaction he'd been wasting his time. When Wilde looked up, the man had already turned on his heel and was making for the door.

'I guess eating can wait,' Tindale said over his shoulder, as he stepped out into the sunshine. 'All that money's making me nervous. The sooner it's where it belongs, the better I'll like it.'

And then Tindale was gone. Sitting back again, reaching for the makings,

Thornton Wilde listened to the sound of the grey gelding's hoofs hammering up the hill; listened to them fade; listened to the familiar, swelling murmur of the town, and with narrowed eyes replayed in his mind the marshal's parting words.

'*The sooner it's where it belongs, the better I'll like it*,' was what Tindale had said. Not back where it belongs — but *where* it belongs. What was he, Wilde, to make of that? Was the other man's choice of words of any consequence? After all, *back where it belongs* and *where it belongs* could both refer to the San Angelo bank. On the other hand, while the first words were unambiguous, the second were open to various interpretations. For instance, Wilde thought, a dishonest man might figure the money belonged anywhere *except* in the San Angelo bank. And if they'd been spoken by anyone other than a fine, upstanding town marshal, well . . .

Pondering, Thornton Wilde struck a match, applied it to his cigarette, blew a jet of smoke towards the ceiling. As he did so, through the open door he heard the beat of hoofs and watched two men ride by. Travel worn. Slouching in the saddle, battered Stetsons pulled down, hard faces unshaven. Eyes constantly moving — and for one moment, as they passed, Wilde thought he saw them glance towards the jail. Then he grinned and shook his head. Hell, most men did that in a furtive way when passing any jail. No, damn it, *all* men did that, at the same time saying a silent prayer of thanks that they were on the outside looking in.

And with the realization that a day that had begun with a mislaid tin badge was making him uncommonly nervous, Thornton Wilde rose to his feet again and went through to get to know to his prisoners.

For some reason, before doing so, he unbuckled his gunbelt and hung it on its peg alongside the keys to the cells. It was a foolish, unthinking act, and one he would live to regret.

2

'You don't recognize me, do you?'

Both men were lying back on thin corn husk mattresses, fingers laced behind their heads. The younger man had spoken as Wilde came through from the office and approached his cell. An emotion the marshal couldn't pin down was darkening the young man's blue eyes. He was waiting for a reaction, but that was something Wilde wasn't prepared to give — at least not until he'd searched through the rusting cells of his memory.

'Should I?'

'Don't let the name fool you. I go by the name of the Waco Kid, and that's all Tindale knows. Makes no difference anyway. All names can be changed. Appearances also change, with time, and we're talking twenty years or more since you last saw me.'

‘Twenty years ago,’ Wilde said, ‘I was marshal of this town. If you passed through then you’d have been, what? Five years old? I reckon you would have looked a mite different.’

‘I didn’t pass through. And I was probably four, though about that I’m uncertain. I told you it could be twenty years or even more, so now I’m saying that four could be three, or even two. Two years old, that’s still a baby — right? Now, are you going to tell me the situation I’m presenting means nothing to you?’

There was a table in the area between the cells. Feeling a creeping numbness, Wilde hastily grabbed one of the chairs. He scraped it back, sat down hard. As he did so, he heard a hoarse chuckle. The older man, Gus Allman, was watching him. He’d fired up a cigarette, and his teeth were bared in a cruel grin.

‘You’ve got him, Lucas boy. I think you’ve just wrote our ticket out of here.’

‘We don’t need a ticket,’ the younger man said, the man Thornton Wilde had been told called himself the Waco Kid. His eyes were still fixed on the marshal when he said, 'Our ticket's booked, you know that. We'll be out of here by sundown.'

'Lucas?' Wilde said. 'Is that your name?'

'Richard. Lucas for short. You should know. You gave it to me.'

Wilde took a deep breath, leaned back and crossed his legs with what he knew was an unconvincing show of nonchalance.

'So let me fill in some details. This *time* we're talking about, this twenty years or some ago — this was in southern Texas? If so, then that would be the time my wife walked out on me with nothing but the clothes on her back. Took my son with her all the way to New York City.'

'Took *me: I'm* your son.'

Thornton Wilde thought about that, about the long arm of coincidence that would have been needed to make the kid's story true, then shook his head.

'No. This has to be a trick, a ruse too clever for me to understand — '

'Go look in the mirror,' the older man said. 'Then come back and say that again.'

The man's words were so portentous, but at the same time so persuasive, that Wilde was shocked into silence. And it took no more than a further few moments' thought before he was forced to tighten his lips and nod. It was a nod of acceptance, because no mirror was needed. The remarkable likeness had struck him outside the jail, the moment he got a close look at the young man — but he had not realized then that what he was looking at was the face he peered at bleary-eyed each morning when he shaved. With the years pared away. Thornton Wilde as a young Texas lawman, a hard man, fast with a gun, who had lost his wife and child because of an obsessive dedication to his job.

The shock was immense. Mind-numbing. He understood, accepted the obvious truth in what he'd been told, but because it was too much for a man to assimilate he was pushing the knowledge into the background and trying to recall other words which, in the circumstances, were of greater importance. What had Allman said? Something about a ticket out of there? The Waco Kid — Wilde closed his eyes — *Lucas* had said they didn't need one because . . .

Wilde opened his eyes. His son, the son he hadn't seen for more than twenty years, was watching and waiting.

'What did you mean,' Wilde said softly, 'when you said you'd be out of here by — ?'

The final word went unuttered as Wilde broke off. He'd been stopped by a distant crash that he knew was the front door being kicked open. The closer sound of feet pounded across the office. Then there was another crash as the same boot hit the door between office and cell block and it burst open.

And even as Thornton Wilde turned away from the Waco Kid's cell and his right hand moved with lightning speed towards his hip and touched only rough cloth, he was remembering two men glancing across as they rode past the jail, and his hand reaching up to hang his gunbelt on its usual wooden peg.

* * *

The door smashed back against the wall. Two tall men crowded through the narrow doorway, guns drawn. One, keys jingling in his free hand, swiftly weighed-up the situation and made for Allman's cell. The other turned towards Thornton Wilde, pistol held high, dark eyes glittering with menace.

'Leave him be,' the Waco Kid called.

The newcomer's thin mouth twitched. He stepped close to Wilde, took a bunch of shirt in his fist, spun him bodily and rammed the muzzle of his pistol hard into the bone behind the marshal's ear. He grinned wolfishly through the bars at the Waco Kid.

'I'm not listening, friend,' he said for

the kid's benefit, 'because you've not yet earned the right to tell me what to do.'

Allman's cell door swung open with a metallic clang. The lean bank robber came out in a rush. He spat onto the dirt floor as the man who had freed him moved to the next cell. Again a key grated in a lock. Waco slipped off his bunk.

'Wait.'

The gunman holding Thornton Wilde snapped the command. His voice cracked like a whip. All movement stopped. In the sudden stillness he nodded towards the Waco Kid.

'Why take him with us?'

The man with the keys looked over his shoulder and sneered.

'Because we need a fast gun, Ryan, and you ain't it.'

'You're dreaming. A fancy name doesn't make a fast gun. He comes up to us after we rob the bank, tells us he's the Waco Kid, rides a flea-bitten nag yet expects us to believe he's greased lightnin' with a six-gun. Next thing we know is he's got himself caught cold by a two-bit town marshal.'

'So when we got to El Paso we should have stayed together — '

'That wasn't the way Gomez had it planned — '

'Gomez had no choice. He's the man in the middle, and you know it. He's the link to — '

'Shut up.'

Allman swung ferociously on the two arguing gunmen. The pistol bit painfully into Wilde's neck as the man holding him jerked with shock, and suddenly Wilde became aware that the grey-haired Allman was the group's leader.

'Jago, turn that key, open the door and let him out,' Allman said. 'And while you're doing that, and until we're well out of here, keep your goddamn mouth shut. That goes for every one of you. Too much said is too much given away — and there's too much at stake.'

Breath hissed angrily, but Ryan, the

man holding the pistol to Wilde's ear, stepped back and watched sullenly as Jago opened the cell door and the Waco Kid walked free.

Already moving towards the door to the office, Allman said, 'On your way out, take your pick of rifles, shotguns, whatever you can find out there.'

'But before that,' Ryan growled, 'we slow down the pursuit,' and with a fierce grin he flipped his pistol, caught it by the barrel and slammed the butt into the base of Thornton Wilde's skull.

3

They rode west, pushing hard towards the Diablo Plateau. By nightfall they had pulled a trail of dust fully forty miles and were well into the foothills of the Delaware mountains. To the north, the soaring heights of Guadalupe Peak were painted a ruddy gold by the last rays of the setting sun. Ahead of them, the rising moon already glinted white on the flat pans of the salt lakes.

There had been no sign of pursuit, and for that Waco was taking the credit. After Ryan had downed the town marshal with a fierce blow to the head, Waco had locked him in one of the cells. The keys had gone with him when they rode out of town, and a mile later had been disposed of in thick brush choking the bed of a dry wash.

Now, with the horses too tired to be driven any further, it was Waco who made tactful suggestions that led to a halt being called. The chosen camp was in a clearing surrounded by thick woods. A rocky bluff protected their rear, and in daylight — should they remain there — they would have an open aspect affording fine views to the east. They cooked supper over a smokeless fire. Then, with moonlight filtering through the trees, they sat around the flames and listened to Allman.

* * *

'First off,' Allman said, 'is we figure out what to do about Tindale. Tindale's got the cash, a total of thirty thousand bucks from three bank robberies. That's a fact. Now, Waco was with me when we heard Tindale tell the Cedar Creek marshal he was taking that cash back to San Angelo. If that was his intention, we've been riding in opposite directions, but Waco doesn't believe that — right, Waco?'

Lucas Wilde, the Waco Kid, was sitting cross-legged close to the fire. Light from the flames flickered on the flat planes of his face, glinted in his pale-blue eyes. He was poking idly at the edge of the glowing embers with a broken stick as he wondered if any of these men he had thrown in his lot with had a single ounce of sense.

'Tindale's out there, ahead of us,' he said, glancing across at Allman. 'He had no intention of taking that cash back to San Angelo, or any other bank. When he left town he rode west, heading for the Mex border at El Paso.'

Allman was twisting strands of his lank greying hair in his fingers, clearly not happy.

'There's something wrong, something we're not seeing. I agree Tindale wants the cash for himself, his lust for it was in his manner, in his eyes. But the man caught us and got his hands on that money in El Paso. If he was planning on crossing into Mexico, why not throw us in jail there — in a goddamn *border* town, for Christ's sake — instead of leading us on the end of a rope a hundred and fifty miles back as far as Cedar Creek? He could have saved himself, what, six days?'

'His intentions were honourable, but he was fighting a losing battle with his conscience,' Waco said.

'An honourable man would have ridden with a posse.'

'The seeds of doubt were there from the outset. He was playing by the rules, but he's a greedy man; by ruling out a posse he left the door open. Once he'd picked us up he set out to take the money back where it belonged, but all the time those damn bills were burning a hole in his saddle-bags and the knowledge finally wore him down. He broke, gave up the fight and dumped us in the nearest town — which happened to be Cedar Creek.'

Allman pulled a face. 'So my hunch is wrong, and I should stop worrying?'

Before Waco could answer, another voice cut in.

'No. Your hunch is right, but you're worrying about the wrong man.'

That was Ryan, glowering darkly from across the fire. His unshaven countenance looked even blacker in the flickering light of the flames. He was reclining, propped on both elbows, his holster pulled around to the front of his thigh so that his six-gun was close to his right hand. But his position made a fast draw impossible, and Lucas Wilde allowed himself a small half smile.

His amusement wasn't lost on Allman.

'If you're referring to our young friend here,' he said, 'I think he'd be inclined to argue.'

'I'd pay more attention to the protests of a donkey. I've already made my feelings plain. That kid waltzed up to us when we'd snatched the cash, horned in on an operation that was going well without him. Threw in a name sounds like it belongs to some fancy Englishman — '

'My grandfather was English,' Waco said.

'Right, then what's this Waco business?' Ryan said, rounding on him. 'A name supposed to transform you into some hot-shot gunslinger? You fooled Jago into believing you're the fastest gun this side of the Mississippi and expect to be treated like God — '

He broke off. Waco hadn't moved — yet there had been a silky whisper of sound and now his pistol was out and levelled at Ryan. The butt was cold and hard and familiar in Waco's palm. With the same economy and speed of movement he spun the pistol, let it smack cleanly into the supple leather holster and lifted his hand as if to scratch his chin. Then, as Jago stared wide-eyed through the smoke hanging over the fire and uttered a breathy 'Jesus Christ' and Ryan began to shake his head, Waco again made the smooth draw that was almost impossible to see.

'I could waste lead clipping the lobes of both your ears, then sit back and watch the blood drip on your shoulders,' he said conversationally, 'but the shots would alert the pursuit — and they will come after us, mark my words.'

'Who will?'

That was Jago, the thin man with a lined face and dark eyes who had opened the cell doors and who, until now, had been silently watching and listening.

'Your father will be riding after us, right?' he went on. 'Your father, the Marshal of Cedar Creek.' He glanced across at Allman. 'Does that inspire confidence? Knowing we've got a lawman's son in our midst?'

'I see no cause for concern,' Allman said dismissively. 'Chance brought them together. You heard them talking before we broke out. They hadn't seen each other in more than twenty years. And didn't Waco stand by and do nothing when Ryan pistol-whipped his pa?'

Jago shook his head. 'I'm with Ryan: I don't trust the Kid.'

Allman studied the faces on the other side of the fire, spread his hands and turned to Waco.

'So, what about that? Will it be your pa coming after us?'

'Probably. No, make that a certainty.'

Waco had been listening, pistol still in his hand, pointing to the skies. Now he pouched it, watched Ryan roll over to lie on his side in disgust.

'And when your father tracks us down,' Allman said, 'and there's a showdown — which side do you take?'

'The side I was with when I rode with you out of San Angelo. The side I was with when Tindale caught us cold in El Paso.' He grinned. 'The side that's going to make me a rich man.'

Allman shook his head. 'That's only part right. The money from San Angelo is going into a big pot, and only a portion of that pot is ours. The bulk of it goes to finance a dream.'

'Yours?'

'Let's say I hitched my wagon to a star; all of us did.'

'Then if I'm to do the same,' Wilde said, 'maybe you'd better tell me exactly what I'm getting into.'

4

The burly town blacksmith was needed to break into the cell holding the bruised and bleeding Thornton Wilde. He was called, perhaps inevitably, by Gord Bogan, who seemed that day to be keeping a watchful eye on the town marshal. Noticing Wilde's unusual absence when the bunch of hard men had thundered out of town in a cloud of dust, he had gone to investigate, and raised the alarm.

When the door to the cell finally creaked open, the blacksmith's beefy face was streaming with perspiration, his white teeth bared in a delighted grin. Over and over he had repeated gleefully as he worked, 'I don't believe it, I really do not believe what I'm doing'. Now, as he led the way through from the cell block to the office with his canvas bag of tools clanking against his leg and saw the black-suited figure waiting in the marshal's swivel chair, the merriment was switched off. He averted his gaze and hurried into the street, a muscular man escaping from an uncomfortable atmosphere created by a small man with an inflated opinion of his own importance.

The pistol-whipping at the hands of the man called Ryan had left Wilde with a splitting headache, and it was with a feeling of foreboding that he watched the big man leave. The blacksmith had left the office door open. The early afternoon sun beat down on the street. Waves of dry, dusty heat rolled into the office. Feeling the instant prickle of perspiration, Wilde placed his big fist against his nose to suppress a sneeze, then carefully shook his aching head and turned to face his visitors.

'A fine mess,' Oliver Shank said, swivelling in Wilde's chair. 'I warned Marshal Tindale he was making a mistake, but he insisted. When he hears about this he'll realize he left his prisoners in the hands of the wrong man.'

'The right man being your son,' Wilde said, and he leaned back wearily against the wall to stare with open contempt at the young man sitting in one of the hard chairs. Aitken Shank had his thumbs hooked into the armholes of his fancy cowhide vest. He toted an ivory-handled pistol in a tooled-leather holster, wore a white Stetson mysteriously unstained by sweat or dust, and at twenty years of age figured he could do a better job of town marshal than Wilde.

'As of today,' Oliver Shank said, 'he's the man wearing the badge. You've made your last cock-up. Aitken's Cedar Creek's new town marshal, so hand over the tin.'

'First cock-up,' Wilde said, 'in more than twenty years of marshalling. The tin stays where it is until I'm voted out.'

Shank shook his head. 'In the event of a disastrous dereliction of duty I'm empowered — '

'The *council's* empowered, not you,'

Wilde said. 'Your first step is to call an extraordinary meeting if you want me out of office.'

'I'm cutting corners to avoid what would be a pointless waste of time.'

'That's the first sensible thing you've said: you know you'd be overruled, so don't waste *my* time when I've got work to do.'

'If I say you're out of a job — '

'I'm not, and as I'm still marshal of this town that leaves decisions pertaining to law enforcement firmly in my hands. I told you I've got work to do. That work is hunting down bank robbers who escaped from my jail. It'll take time, I'll be away from town for several days — '

'Leaving Cedar Creek without an officer of the law — '

'No. If you want your boy to get a taste of what it takes to police a small town, I'll deputize him here and now. You and the other councillors can keep your eye on him, see how he shapes up. Then, when I get back . . . '

Wilde watched father and son exchange glances, saw the boy's chest swell visibly, and felt mild amusement as he followed their train of thought and knew they figured that once the badge was pinned on Aitken Shank's fancy vest it would be difficult to remove.

'Good thinking, Marshal,' Shank said. 'Pin that badge on my boy and townsfolk will know they're looking at the next marshal of their town — '

'Deputy marshal, for a trial period.'

Dismissing the correction with a haughty gesture, Shank ploughed on, 'You've made the right decision, but as leader of the town council I must express my misgivings at your intentions. I get the impression you don't intend to raise a posse. Going after that bunch of hardcases without the help of armed men is asking for trouble.'

'I'll take one man. A deputy.'

'Your deputy's laid low with a broken leg.'

'I had another man in mind.'

'Who?'

And that was where Wilde was stumped. Battling against the ache in his head, beset by images of a callow youth strutting through the town wearing a shiny badge, he racked his brains and was unable to come up with a suitable candidate. Oliver Shank was watching him with a knowing smirk. Aitken Shank was looking around the office, clearly surveying the territory which would soon be his domain. Seconds ticked by. Oliver Shank moved restlessly, opened his mouth —

'I, er, I . . . ' Wilde said — and then, to his immense relief, a familiar tall figure appeared, ambling unsteadily past the open street door.

'Gord,' Wilde roared, as Bogan's long shadow fell across the dusty boards.

Gord Bogan came to a swaying halt and peered into the office.

'Gord, can you climb aboard a horse, ride for more than a mile at a time without falling off?'

'I guess I can, Marshal, at a push,' Bogan said, his eyes mystified.

'And can you fire a pistol without plugging yourself in the foot or any other part of your anatomy?'

Bogan's blue eyes crinkled, his grin was crooked.

'I can fire a pistol,' he said, 'without hitting a barn door or the barn itself.'

'Damn it, you'll do. Get inside here. You're about to be sworn in as deputy marshal.'

5

Darkness was creeping across the eastern plains when Wilde and Gord Bogan rode out of Cedar Creek. Wilde was on his big sorrel, Bogan on a rangy buckskin. They pointed their mounts towards the flame-red sunset streaking the western skies, pushed on hard, and by midnight had covered more than thirty miles. That carried them close to the foothills of the Delaware Mountains, and Wilde was faced with a dilemma. He glanced across at the indistinct shape of his new deputy, riding a couple of yards behind, and flung an arm out to the right. Then, swinging his mount off the trail, he called a halt.

'The way I read it,' he said, when they had ground-tethered their horses in a patch of sweet grass and hunkered down with water bottles and glowing cigarettes, 'is those bank robbers will be cock-a-hoop, see themselves as untouchable. That being the case, they'll be rolled up in their blankets alongside a glowing camp-fire with maybe one of them standing guard — and he'll be nodding off. And if our pace has matched theirs, and we keep on riding, we're likely to overrun their encampment and find ourselves in a heap of trouble.'

Bogan's eyes gleamed in the faint light of the rising moon.

'Isn't catching them what we set out to do? And won't the element of surprise work in our favour?'

'We aim to catch them at a time and place of our choosing, not full dark out in the open or, worse, deep in thick timber.'

'Letting sleeping dogs lie,' Bogan said, 'could see them slipping away like thieves in the night.'

'You're full of surprises, Gord. Got the look of a hobo, talk like a man who got himself a degree from Yale.'

'Funny you should say that,' Bogan said. 'I studied there for a year before boredom set in. Got fed up and did exactly what we've been talking about.'

'Slipped away?'

'Upped sticks.'

'For Cedar Creek?'

'Let's say that's where I lost my way.'

Wilde puffed on his cigarette, squinted across at the dim, Indian-dark figure sitting cross-legged with his back against the bole of a tree. Looked sober — but the man could hold his drink, and Wilde hadn't been there when he filled his water bottle. He'd been steady on his horse, too. But many westerners were practically born in the saddle. Well, time would tell . . .

'So what I've done today is what?' Wilde said. 'Thrown a lifeline to a drowning man? Offered a man without a future a glimmer of hope?'

'It was me made me a drunk, Marshal — '

'Thorn.'

Bogan nodded. 'I made me a drunk,

Thorn, so it's up to me to turn myself around.'

'My offer came out of the blue — surprised me as well as you — but by accepting it I'd say you took a first step in the right direction.'

Bogan's teeth gleamed in a grin.

'Maybe, but it's one that could get me killed.'

'Not by sitting here aimlessly chewing the fat. We need a plan, Gord. Any ideas?'

'Let me ask you a question: how do you know we're heading in the right direction? How do you know the tracks we've been following were cut into the trail by the four horses carrying those bank robbers, and not just any four riders?'

'I don't. Not for sure. But we picked them up in Cedar Creek, they're pointing in the general direction of the Mex border and never strayed from that line, so what's your point?'

'I'm part Indian. And I *know* we're following the right men, because one of them has been talking to me ever since we rode out.'

Wilde rolled his eyes. 'Right. You're being guided by spirits?'

Gord chuckled. 'No. By a man who's probably risking his life leaving signs on the trail I've been smart enough to spot.'

'What kind of signs?'

'Broken saplings showing white wood. Flattened grass in a place where it couldn't be trodden on by man nor beast. A stick on the trail, looking like it's been carelessly dropped, but pointing the way.'

The question that at once entered Wilde's mind was, which one of the outlaws was laying the trail? The answer he wanted — that the man assisting them was his long lost son — was something he barely dared contemplate for fear of being wrong.

'So you noticed those signs, but didn't think to share this with me? Left me with my nose to the ground struggling to follow impressions in the trail about as distinct as those made by dead leaves falling on hard sand.'

'You already had your mind made up about where they were headed.' Gord shrugged. 'Anyway, one method's as good as another. If we succeed in tracking down the bank robbers, who's to say which one of us got there?'

'For a drunk,' Wilde said, 'you come up with some pretty sobering thoughts.'

'*Profound* thoughts,' Gord Bogan corrected, grinning. 'And if your remark was intended as a joke, Thorn, my advice is to try much harder — '

He broke off as distant gunfire rattled, and somewhere on the other side of the woods muzzle flashes flickered like lightning.

'I think you said he was risking his life,' Wilde said. He spoke softly, but it was with a sense of despair for which he could find no reasonable explanation. 'I still don't know who we've been talking about, but by the sound of that I think the man who's been showing us the way has been consigned to history.'

And, even as he spoke, with two final, booming explosions the distant guns fell silent. To Wilde, it was the silence of the grave.

* * *

'What you're getting into,' Gus Allman said, 'is the beginning of one Mexican's campaign to reclaim Texas for his country.'

The fire was dying, the blackened coffee pot lying on its side in the dull embers. Looking through the thin veil of smoke, Lucas Wilde, the Waco Kid, could see Ryan under the trees. An indistinct figure in dappled shadows cast by the pale moon, he was once again lying on his back so that he could watch as well as listen. Waco thought he saw the surly gunman's eyes narrow at Allman's words, and he wondered if that reaction was out of disbelief that the lean man calling the shots would take Waco into his confidence.

Waco's own mind was racing. In San

Angelo he had worked his way into a perilous situation in which he was encircled by dangerous outlaws who looked on him with suspicion. That act had been either courageous or foolhardy, but his assumed outlaw identity, the reputation that went with it and his conduct since joining the outlaw band had gone some way to allaying those suspicions. Now it seemed that his risky infiltration was about to pay off. By taking Waco into his confidence, Allman was tacitly admitting the kid was now a member of the outlaw band — but Waco knew that the other two men had strong misgivings, and so there was still a need for caution.

'Are you throwing dust in my eyes?' he said. 'Texas is part of the Union. Take on Texas, you take on the United States.'

'This is no joke. All the bank robberies were masterminded by Charlie Gomez — '

'All?'

'San Angelo was the third,' Allman

said, 'and in each one, Charlie Gomez was acting on the orders of Paco Ibañez. Ibañez was born into a poor farming community in the Sonora region of Mexico, but he has big ideas. His parents were murdered by a gang of marauding Texas outlaws. Grief at his loss festered, and turned into hatred of all things American, but especially Texan. He's studied history, read extensively of the fighting in Texas back in the 1830s, and reveres the name of Antonio López de Santa Anna — '

'Ibañez is modelling himself on that dictator?'

'He believes that Texas belongs rightfully to Mexico. If regaining it requires a man with the powers enjoyed by Santa Anna, he's prepared to take on that role.'

'But he needs cash?'

Allman grinned. 'You catch on fast.'

'So why you fellows? Why would a bunch of red-blooded Texans work for Charlie Gomez and a Mexican peasant intent on overthrowing their country?'

'I got to know Charlie in the pen. He was serving time for slitting the throat of a man who thought he was easy meat. Did a couple of years, and in all that time he never lost touch with Ibañez. I reckon it was about then they got to cooking up this grand scheme.'

'And recruited you and your friends?'

'Going to Texas to raise the money to get things moving makes sense, and gives the story a wry twist: Texas helps finance its own downfall.' He grinned. 'It also means there's less chance of discovery. In Texas, bank robberies are a fact of life. So Ibañez gets his cash, yet, in the eyes of Mexican authorities who would surely oppose his scheme, he's got clean hands.'

Across the fire, Ryan coughed, then heaved his big frame up off the grass and approached the fire.

'You're talking too much, Gus,' he said, hunkering down and stretching out his palms to the meagre warmth.

'I don't think so. After all, we're all in the same boat. Like it or not, Waco's one of us. Every damn one of us spends the best part of his life on the run. Why? Because we're all wanted by the law. That law is Texas law, the stinking holes we've sweated in were Texas jails. Waco asked a sensible question. My answer is, if we can line our pockets with cash and change our lives by overthrowing a government that's given us nothing but pain — let's do it.'

Jago had again been listening in watchful silence. Now he cleared his throat, spat towards the dying fire.

'Your thinking is way off, Gus. Sure, riding with Ibañez is the way to go, but Waco can't be part of it. I go along with Ryan: everything changed when you were locked up in Cedar Creek, because that was when you found out Waco's the son of a lawman.' Lithely, he came to his feet, took a step back from the fire. 'Waco was asking questions, Gus. I think he was digging for information for his own ends. Now I'd like to ask some of Waco — and, one way or another, his answers will settle this.'

'Cool down, and back off,' Allman said. 'The man wants to know what's going on. If I was in his position, I'd be asking questions.'

Jago stared at Waco. 'Is that right?'

'You heard me tell Gus: I need to know what I'm getting into.'

'You already knew that when you joined. You could see we operate on the wrong side of the law: you watched us rob the bank in San Angelo. You were happy to tag along with a bunch of bank robbers. What more do you need to know?'

'At the time, nothing, and that's why I rode with you to El Paso. But Gus and the man called Gomez talked secretively for most of the journey. Then, in El Paso, Gomez slipped away. Less than an hour later we were caught cold by Tindale.'

Jago grinned mirthlessly. 'What d'you reckon to that, Gus? Me, I'd say he's trying to wriggle out of a tight situation by casting suspicion on a man who ain't here to defend himself. Or on you. The tight situation is that he's under suspicion himself, and I reckon the more he talks the deeper he's digging himself into a hole.'

Allman snorted. 'So far he's doing nothing but tell the truth. Gomez and me, we did do a lot of talking on that long ride. And Gomez did walk away from us in El Paso — we know why, Waco doesn't, so it's no wonder he's a mite chary. The way I see it, he's on the level, so make your point or shut up and sit down.'

'On the level?' Jago's eyes were ugly. 'You believe that then you're blind or stupid, Gus. While you and Ryan have been riding with your eyes shut and your mind on all the money you're going to make, I've been watching what's been going on around me. This so-called Waco Kid has been leaving signs on the trail for his pa that make following us as easy as walking down Cedar Springs' main street on a sunny afternoon.'

There was a sudden, ominous silence.

In the deathly hush an owl hooted, its haunting cry answered by the whinny of a horse that, in Lucas Wilde's estimation, was close but not close enough to save his bacon. He saw Allman shoot a glance at Ryan, who had tensed as he cocked his head to listen for the sound of hoofs that would mean the pursuit was closing in. Jago was nodding, his eyes gleaming at what appeared to be vindication of his suspicions. He had moved even further back from the fire, and his right hand was like an eagle's claw ready to snatch at the butt of his six-gun.

'Think before you act, Allman,' the Waco Kid said. 'If sign's been left on the trail — and you've only got Jago's word for it — then either Jago or Ryan could be double-crossing you and pushing the blame onto me.'

'Yeah, and who am I supposed to believe?' Allman said. 'You, or the two men I've been riding with for the past couple of years? Damn it, Waco, I've got to know you, got around to trusting you

— thought for sure you were the hardened gunslinger who came out of nowhere to add strength to the group — '

Ryan's laugh was mocking. Allman glared.

' — add strength, fire power, help us through the fighting that lies ahead when Ibañez makes the move across the border into Texas.'

He stood up, swung an angry kick at the fire and sent smoking embers flying. Looked at Ryan; looked at Jago; then swung on Waco.

'So, which is it? Expert gunslinger, tagged onto a bunch of bank robbers and discovered he'd become involved in a heroic revolution? Or a lawman's son who'd got wind of what's about to happen and figured the best, the *only* way of ripping up the plans, is from the inside?'

'I've said my piece,' Waco said softly. 'Now it's for you to decide.'

Allman grimaced. 'Jago?'

'I saw what I saw: the man's a traitor.'

Allman hesitated for a fraction of a second. Then he shook his head and, as swiftly as a cat, dived sideways and rolled away from the fire.

Waco leaped to his feet and, with the same blinding speed, whirled and drew his six-gun. His first shot cracked, kicking up dust and leaves close to Allman's head. His second plucked at Jago's sleeve. Then Ryan's six-gun spat flame. Waco leaped sideways, felt the wind of the shot. He dropped to a crouch, turned one way then the other, looked frantically for a way out and knew he was up against a well-oiled team. All three men had backed away, giving themselves space and leaving him in the centre of a triangle of danger with nowhere to go. As Waco snapped a third shot, directing it at Ryan, bullets tore at him from three different directions.

In the darkness, the muzzle flashes were dazzling. Waco was disorientated by the bright flashes of light. Exploding gunpowder crackled. Hot lead hissed close to his head. But hammering at him was the notion that if he was going to extricate himself he should take on one man, not three. Knowing he was staring death in the face, Waco took the one action that could save his life. Jago stood between him and the stand of trees where they had tethered the horses. With a fierce roar, Waco charged straight at the thin gunman.

He ran hard, jinking from side to side, six-gun blazing. Jago's hat flew from his head. His eyes widened, showing the whites. Waco saw him rock backwards, undecided. Then, desperately, the outlaw threw himself sideways. He hit the ground hard. Rolling, he fought to bring his six-gun to bear on his attacker. Waco bore down on him. Hastily, Jago snatched at the trigger. The shot was wild. The bullet whined harmlessly into the trees. Grinning savagely, Waco leaped over the prostrate outlaw. He felt a hand grasp his ankle, kicked out hard then sprinted towards the horses.

'He's getting away,' Allman roared.

Waco heard Ryan curse, then the thud of boots and the crackle of leaves and branches. Allman and Ryan were coming after him, snapping shots as they ran. Waco was still thirty yards from the horses, but closing fast. The animals were frantic with terror. Rolling their eyes, they backed away, frantically tugging at the rope tethers. The gunfire was driving them crazy with fear but, using his head, Waco now ran straight at the four panicking mounts. He had placed himself directly between horses and outlaws. A bullet that whistled past him would almost certainly hit one of the rearing mounts. The guns fell silent.

Ten long strides and Waco reached his horse. He always used a quick release knot when tethering his mount. Now, one sharp jerk and the reins fell free. Clutching them in one hand he flung himself into the saddle and flattened himself along the horse's neck. He kicked hard with his heels, at the same time using soft words to urge the animal around and into the woods. Clouds were drifting across the moon, and his aim was to put solid timber between himself and the gunmen's bullets. If he covered the first fifty yards or so unscathed he was confident that in the blackness of night he would make his escape.

But undergrowth slowed his progress. The horse was forced to high-step, jinking left and right through the trees, sometimes backing and taking a different path when the way forward was blocked. Acutely aware of silence behind him, Waco bared his teeth in a silent grimace of frustration as he guessed Allman's intentions.

Instead of engaging in a futile pursuit, the outlaw would be slipping his rifle out of its saddle boot, steadying himself against a tree and attempting to shoot Waco out of the saddle.

His fears were justified. The forest thickened. The horse was forced to slow to a hesitant walk. Brush crackled beneath its hoofs as it tossed its head, snorted, tried to back and turn. And suddenly a deep boom followed by the snick of a branch being severed told Waco that the rifle Allman favoured was a big one, probably a percussion Hawken.

The mountain rifle was single shot — but Waco's desperate situation gave Allman all the time in the world. Forced upright in the saddle, fighting against the horse's desire to turn and make for open ground, Waco found himself side on to the gunman's position. In his sudden fear he could almost hear Allman working at the breech, inserting the fresh load, fitting the percussion cap. Tugging at the reins, trying to force the reluctant horse to push on through the woods, he found himself counting the seconds. He reached five, then ten —

He didn't hear the sound of the second shot. A tremendous blow on the back almost knocked him from the saddle. He fell forward, clutching for the mane, the muscular neck, but all the time his senses were failing and before his hands could reach their objective the darkness enveloped him and his last memory was of a sensation of falling into a bottomless pit that was as cold as ice.

6

It had been intended as a brief halt to gather their thoughts and come up with ideas, so there was no camp to break in frantic haste. Almost before those two heavy explosions had rolled into silence like distant thunder, Thornton Wilde and Gord Bogan had flung themselves into the saddle and were on the trail heading west at a fast clip. In the thin moonlight, Wilde swiftly pulled ahead of his deputy, spurring his sorrel like a man possessed. He was tormented by the conviction that his son, the Waco Kid, had been the target for the volley of shots. His mind was haunted by a vision of the dark young man falling from his horse, his body riddled with bullets.

Riding with the ease of a born horseman, Gord Bogan effortlessly pulled level and rode his buckskin in close enough for stirrups to clash.

'Camp-fire not too far ahead and away to the right.'

'Your ancestors' spirits talking to you again?'

'I can smell smoke. And the breeze is from the north-west.'

'Yeah, and if I'm not mistaken I can hear a bunch of horses. Whoever's on 'em's riding away from here like bats out of hell.'

'You're right — but there was a reason for that gunfire, and it's telling me they're down to three men.'

Because Wilde's son was one of those men, Bogan's words sent an icy chill rippling through his soul. Grim faced, the marshal ducked his head, the wind flattening his hat brim as he rode on. And now his nostrils had picked up the scent of the camp-fire. Bogan had been right, the breeze was carrying the smoke across the woods from the north-west. But should they push through the timber, or go round? Skirting the woods was the longer way, but could be quicker —

Before he could open his mouth to give the order, Bogan had pulled away from him and was hammering along the edge of the woods. The trail took a wide swing to the right. As they followed that broad sweep, the marshal caught another scent mingled with the smoke. Then, ahead on the trail he saw a haze of dust settling in the pale moonlight, caught the fading drumbeat of hoofs as the outlaws made their getaway.

'There,' Bogan called, flinging an arm right and reining in so hard the buckskin slid to a halt in a cloud of dust with braced forelegs and a shrill whinny of protest.

Wilde rode on by, swinging in the direction his deputy had indicated as Bogan fought to stay in the saddle and control his agitated mount. He rode into a clearing beneath a sheer rocky bluff, swiftly noted the dying fire, the signs of a hurried departure: a blackened coffee pot on its side in the embers, a blanket dragged in haste then left in the dust and, close to the fringe of woods marking the clearing's perimeter, a man's Stetson.

'If they're down to three as you suggest,' Wilde said as Bogan trotted in to join him at the fire, 'where's the fourth?'

As if in reply, the marshal's sorrel whinnied softly, and swung its head towards the woods. There was an answering whinny, the crackle of twigs.

The two men exchanged swift glances. Then Wilde swung from the saddle and hit the ground running. But again he was overtaken by his fast moving deputy. By the time Wilde reached the edge of the clearing, Gord Bogan was crashing through the undergrowth to where a horse could be seen, stock still, quivering. As Wilde drew nearer he could see a still figure slumped in the saddle, and was shocked to realize that what was spooking the horse was the raw, coppery scent of blood. Then Bogan had grasped the hanging reins. Whispering, coaxing, he began to turn the horse.

'Wait,' Wilde said sharply. 'Without someone holding him, that feller'll topple over.'

He moved in close enough to reach up, grasped the slumped man's arm and took a firm grip on his belt.

'OK, go ahead.'

Together, with Bogan leading the horse and Wilde steadying the wounded man and at times taking most of his weight, they slow-walked the horse through the undergrowth and out into the clearing. There, back on firm ground and with room to move, they eased the semi-conscious man out of the saddle and down onto the ground close to the camp-fire's still warm embers.

'Find dry sticks, get that fire blazing,' Thornton Wilde said. 'I'll fetch blankets, see what I've got in the way of medical supplies.' He cast a fierce yet imploring glance at Bogan. 'It's exactly what I hoped for, and what I feared the most: it was my son laying that trail, and he's paid for it. But after losing him for a full twenty years through my pig-headed stupidity, I don't intend to repeat that mistake.'

* * *

It took a half-hour of bloody, amateur surgery to remove the bullet from Lucas Wilde's left shoulder. In that relatively short time the kid hung on grimly with the help of a stick to clamp his teeth on and a half-pint bottle of moonshine whiskey Gord Bogan just happened to have in his saddle-bag. And Thornton Wilde, his face carved out of stone, discovered that slicing and probing into his son's flesh with a knife blade cauterized in the flames of the now blazing fire was more terrifying than anything he had ever faced as a lawman.

When it was over, when the slippery chunk of lead from the Hawken mountain rifle had clinked onto a tin plate, Lucas Wilde was propped up by the fire with a feeble grin on his pale face and a blanket draped across his shoulders. Marshal Thornton Wilde felt drained. He sat close to the flames, elbows on spread knees and the almost empty whiskey bottle hanging loosely in a hand that seemed to have lost all his strength.

His mind, however, was still alert.

'Tell me if I'm barking up the wrong tree,' he said, 'but a sixth sense developed over the years is telling me you fellers are acquainted.'

Lucas chuckled. 'Gord's Cedar Creek's town drunk,' he said, his voice weak but steady. 'I'm the notorious Waco Kid. We've got nothing in common.'

'I recall Bogan riding in six months ago. Looked all right to me, yet within a week he was staggering around like an injun on mescal. A man doesn't become a drunk overnight — and, as I recall, there's nary a dodger in my office relating to someone calling himself the Waco Kid.'

He cast a calculating look at his son.

'One man turns into a bum. Another

takes on an identity. Could it be that day six months ago was one of some importance? Like, one when a certain planned sequence of actions was put into effect?'

'For what purpose?' Bogan said, 'and by whom?'

'Yeah, that's sounds like a Yale man talking, which gives some weight to what I'm saying,' Wilde said. He shrugged. 'You've just heard me thinking aloud, making a stab at what might've happened. So why don't you save us some time, and tell me if I'm right?'

'You're right.'

'Thank you. So what are you two? Feds?'

'Texas Rangers,' Bogan said.

'Really?' Wilde said, his voice dryly sceptical. 'Me, I *know* I'm a lawman, and despite what you say my first inclination is to throw my own son in jail. So, tell me a plausible tale. Convince me I'm wrong. Describe the connection between a man playing drunk in a town on the Pecos and another who helps a bunch of no good outlaws rob a bank more than a hundred and fifty miles away in San Angelo.'

7

'We were in Austin when we got wind of a bunch of outlaws,' Gord Bogan said. 'Not just any old wild bunch out to get rich quick, but a bunch who looked like they were aiming much higher. They were working their way west, picking off banks as they rode. It began when they crossed from Louisiana and robbed the bank at Shreveport on the Red River. Next was Waco. They robbed the bank there — and that was on the Brazos. San Angelo was next — '

'On the North Concho,' Wilde said, 'but by then you'd got a man in place.'

He'd rescued the outlaws' blackened pot from the embers and, using his own supplies from his saddle-bag and water from the nearby spring, had brewed fresh coffee. Now, his mind on the story he was hearing, he poured the thick black java into three tin cups.

‘It was a weak chain you were following,’ he said, as he handed the coffee to Lucas, ‘because they could have changed their methods at any time, or simply disappeared. So what I can’t understand is why you two rangers let them run. Why you didn’t arrest them as they walked into the San Angelo bank. And why you, son, as the man in place, stood by while the bank was robbed then worked your way in under an assumed name that would give you some kind of fragile credibility.’

‘We gave them their heads because the way they were operating was out of the ordinary,’ Lucas said, clutching the hot cup in one hand as he pulled the blanket around his shoulders.

Wilde frowned. ‘There has to be more to it than that. Those banks were losing money to men known to the authorities, and no attempt was made to stop them. Hell fire, no bank would stand for that — ’

‘The banks were reimbursed, compensated, whatever you like to call it,’

Bogan said. 'Someone, almost certainly the US Government, decided the cost of repayment was small change compared with what they might discover by giving the outlaws their heads.'

'Which suggests,' Wilde said, 'that the end is important enough to make the means insignificant.'

'We knew they were up to something big all right,' Lucas said, 'but we were left scratching our heads. Also, there was a Mexican with them, Charlie Gomez, and that Mexican was known to us. He was a bad hat, regularly skipping between El Paso and Ciudad Juárez. What he was doing there is another mystery we need to solve, but we do know he works for a Mexican called Paco Ibañez. So, Gomez was involved in those bank robberies and, as the direction they were taking was almost due west — '

'The likelihood is they wouldn't stop until they reached the border,' Thornton finished for him.

'Right. And as they were using banks

located on river towns as their stepping stones to immense riches,' Gord Bogan said, 'it seemed likely they'd rob the bank at El Paso — on the Rio Grande — '

'Or Rio Bravo del Norte, depending on your viewpoint,' Wilde said. 'So if that was the way you read it, why did you choose Cedar Creek as the place to turn to drink?'

'The town's got a bank. It's on the Pecos.' Bogan shrugged. 'It's the one time we figured wrong: they gave your town a miss. Yet, in my estimation, that hasn't changed the outcome: they'll help themselves to one final heap of cash from the El Paso bank — then cross the river into Mexico.'

For a few moments there was silence as all three men savoured their coffee while gazing into the flickering flames. Then Thornton Wilde glanced across at Bogan.

'At which point,' he said softly, 'we come to Marshal Reb Tindale.'

Lucas Wilde chuckled. 'Yeah, Tindale was the maverick we had our eyes on, but plumb forgot. The San Angelo town council knew they'd elected a lawman who liked bending the rules. What they maybe didn't know was he was also a *greedy* lawman tortured by indecision. From the official wires reaching his office he knew what was going on; knew those fellows were robbing a series of banks, and likely to pass through his town on their way to the Mex' border. And the one decision he didn't dither over was his determination to stand by while they robbed his town bank, and see what transpired. What he didn't know was there was a wild card: Lucas was there, waiting to join the bunch at San Angelo — and for obvious reasons, Lucas couldn't tell him.'

'So what Tindale did,' Gord Bogan said, 'was go after those bank robbers. He was out on his lonesome chasing three Texans, one Mexican and an undercover Texas Ranger. All the way to El Paso. Where, in the blink of an eye, he found himself facing just two men. Gomez, Ryan and Jago walked away into the town's mean back streets, leaving me, and Gus Allman who was holding all the cash.'

'Allman being the bunch's honcho,' Wilde said, nodding. 'Least that's what I figured from the way he was acting in the jail.'

'You're right, but the point is, we were caught cold,' Lucas said. 'Tindale showed himself, arrested me and Gus Allman — and the rest you know.'

'Or will do when you tell us what you've learned in the short time you've been with them.' He lifted an eyebrow. 'You up to it?'

'I'm light-headed and aching, like I visited a country fair, stayed on the carousel for a full hour then fell on stony ground.' He grinned, and held out his empty cup. 'But in answer to your question, yes, I am up to it. Give me a refill, then sit back and I'll tell you a story that'll leave both of you enlightened, but confused.'

* * *

Well, Thornton Wilde later reflected, Lucas was certainly right on that score. Talk of a Mexican peasant planning the takeover of Texas would have been laughable if the story Lucas told them hadn't borne the ring of truth, and the thought of Marshal Reb Tindale high-tailing for El Paso, saddle-bags stuffed with cash that was supposed to begin financing an invasion army of Mexican peasants, really did have Thornton and Gord Bogan spluttering into their coffee.

Trouble was, if the story of a Mexican annexation of Texas was all so much bull, what the hell *was* going on? Lucas was convinced Reb Tindale was a maverick lawman on the loose with a heap of cash. If Allman was to be believed, that cash had been illegally acquired on the orders of one Charlie Gomez. Gomez was working for Paco Ibañez.

If the trail ended with Ibañez, then he was the man with the answers. No doubt the two Texas Rangers, Gord

Bogan and Lucas Wilde, would track him down — and he, Thornton Wilde, would go with them. But before they set out on that quest, there was time to indulge in a mental activity Thornton thoroughly enjoyed: the exercise of intelligent speculation.

After telling his story, Lucas Wilde had tired rapidly, and been made comfortable in blankets placed close to the glowing fire. Gord Bogan had settled on the opposite side of the fire, finished off the whiskey — most of which had been used as an anaesthetic — then winked at Thornton Wilde, rolled over and immediately begun snoring. Thornton, happy with his fourth tin cup of coffee, was now stretched out with his head on his saddle, gazing up at the stars.

If Lucas was right they were, he realized, involved in a crazy situation. Tindale was racing for the border with money he'd stolen from a bunch of outlaws, the outlaws were hot on his heels, and they in turn were being followed by two Texas Rangers and a tired old town marshal. It only needed an unknown someone to be following the rangers and one Thornton Wilde, and the crazy situation would become a farce.

That was a fair description of the crazy goings on, but it didn't begin to explain the whys and the wherefores. What it came down to was the idea of a Mexican peasant scheming to annex Texas. It took but a moment's thought for Thornton Wilde to reject that out of hand. It was easy to see Gus Allman being hoodwinked by a talkative Mexican in a Texas jail, and the implausibility of the crackpot scheme wouldn't worry him as long as he was making money. But nobody was about to take over the State of Texas.

With that said, it was back to the unanswered question: what the hell was going on?

Fact. A Mexican peasant named Paco Ibañez was making a lot of money out of a bunch of gullible Texans. He'd invented a death-or-glory grandiose scheme of territorial warfare to get them on his side, when he could simply have said, 'Hey, gringo, I am but a poor Mexican. Go rob some banks for me. We will split the proceeds, and I will give you sanctuary in my country.'

In the starlight, Thornton Wilde chuckled silently, but hard enough to spill his coffee. Christ, never mind Paco Ibañez, now who was letting his imagination run riot? The bank robberies were fact. The jail break was fact. Beyond that, they were struggling, and not just with striving to understand a bizarre situation. The answers they were seeking lay in El Paso and beyond, and Lucas Wilde had been weakened by a heavy chunk of lead that had drilled into his left shoulder. They would be forced to ride at the pace of the slowest member of the group. Inevitably, they would be outdistanced by Reb Tindale and the outlaws.

When they did eventually catch

up — as he was damn sure they would — they'd also be outnumbered, Wilde thought ruefully, and about that there was not a damn thing they could do.

But of course, he was wrong.

8

A hundred miles of rugged terrain lay between the three lawmen and the border town of El Paso. They set out when the sun was a dazzling promise painting the skies above the eastern horizon, knowing that with Lucas Wilde stoically suffering agonies from his injury the best they could hope for was a couple of hours riding between rests, with little more than fifteen miles covered in each two-hour spell.

Each rest period swallowed up another hour. Riding ever more slowly, they reached the end of the hot, dusty, twelve-hour day having put just sixty miles behind them. Not surprisingly, in all that time they had seen nothing of Tindale or the outlaws. Tindale was riding to keep hold of the money he had stolen, and to hang on to his life. The men chasing him would be riding hard, but without undue urgency. They knew the lawman fleeing with the banks' money would be hunted down if he stayed in the United States. If he crossed into Mexico he was a gringo in a land were gringos were fair game, and as good as dead.

When the three lawmen bedded down that night, their second on the trail, Lucas Wilde was flushed, his eyes suspiciously glassy. Thornton Wilde examined his son's wound, merely grunted non-committally when he saw the angry inflammation that suggested infection was taking hold, then dressed it as best he could with the available medical supplies.

By next morning, Lucas was beginning to sound incoherent. Thornton Wilde knew that the infection was causing Lucas's temperature to rise and pushing him towards delirium. And they were still forty miles from El Paso.

They again broke camp early, hoping to get some miles under their belts before the sun got too high. They managed that but, by the midday rest that was taken in the meagre shade of wilting aspens scattered across a dry creek bed, Lucas was drifting in and out of consciousness. He had been riding slumped in the saddle, head lolling, clinging to the horn with both hands with the natural instinct of a born horseman. In unspoken agreement, Thornton Wilde and Gord Bogan had ridden close in on either side of the injured man's big blood bay. If Lucas fell to left or right, the Texas Ranger or the town marshal would be there to support him.

When they set off again in the heat of the afternoon they were, in Wilde's estimation, within twenty miles of El Paso. By Socorro, with ten miles to go, they were riding close to the banks of the Rio Grande, hats tipped back and faced turned to make the most of the cool breeze coming off the rolling waters.

The bracing air revived Lucas Wilde. He was conscious, his eyes were brighter, and he nodded and smiled weakly when Thornton asked how he was feeling. Being realistic, Thornton Wilde allowed himself only a small measure of hope — but it *was* hope. He had regained a son. That son was a member of an elite band of lawmen, and he was on a perilous assignment. Wilde knew, as a father, he couldn't ask for much more. He was so damn proud it was making him embarrassed in case it showed on his face, but at the same time he was scared out of his wits that the boy would be snatched from him before they'd had time to get acquainted. He'd do his best to make sure that didn't happen, but he knew that they were not yet out of the woods. Not yet, and not by a long shot — but, God-willing, by sundown they would be riding into El Paso and putting the Texas Ranger known as Lucas Wilde into the capable hands of a doctor.

9

The first shot came whistling out of the blue. It dropped Gord Bogan's gallant buckskin. The horse went down without uttering a sound, dumping the Texas Ranger in the dust. Even as Thornton Wilde's eyes widened in shock he heard the crack of the rifle. It was followed by shrill, excited cries, and the drum of hoofs along the river-bank to their rear.

'Mexicans,' Bogan yelled. He crawled over and tried to drag his rifle out of its saddle boot. The horse had fallen on that side. The leather scabbard was under its dead weight. Bogan moved to a sitting position, put his boots against the horse and used his leg muscles to pull the rifle free. Then he scrambled to his feet and ran for the cottonwoods fringing the river-bank.

'Lucas, get after Gord and keep your head down,' Wilde roared.

With considerable trepidation he waited until his injured son turned his horse and urged it down the slope after Bogan. Then, spinning his sorrel on the spot, Wilde turned to face the danger.

Four riders. Still almost a quarter mile away. They were spread out, advancing in open line. But not hurrying, Wilde noted. Didn't relish the task. Mindful of Lucas's story, he guessed shrewdly that they were obeying orders. Trying to make life easier for themselves by waving their repeating rifles, screaming themselves hoarse and firing wildly. Hoping to scare off the gringos. Well, they hadn't achieved that, but one of those wild shots had downed Bogan's horse.

Grinning sourly, Wilde again spun his horse and made for the trees at a fast canter.

'Fair odds?' he said to Bogan, swinging out of the saddle and reaching for his rifle.

'Those Mex boys don't know it, but they're in trouble,' Bogan said, and he dropped to one knee, steadied himself against a slim cottonwood and brought his rifle to his shoulder.

'Warn them,' Bogan said. 'They're worried now. Maybe the sound of hot lead whipping by'll be too much to swallow and they'll turn tail.'

Bogan began firing, snapping spaced shots over the heads of the slowly advancing Mexicans. Wilde turned to his son.

'Lucas, in your condition you're best out of this. Turn around now, ride through the trees and out, then keep going for El Paso.'

Lucas, eyes bright, face animated as he sat atop the big blood bay, shook his head firmly.

'You're letting your heart rule your head, Pa,' he said. 'Look to your front. Those Mexicans have split up. If you're not careful they'll be coming at us from front, flank and rear.'

Galvanized by Gord Bogan's steady firing, the Mexicans had stopped their wild shooting and were riding with purpose. Two were bouncing in the saddle as they trotted along the river-bank, without haste, weaving in and out of the sparse cottonwoods. They should have been easy targets, but the river curved behind them and the bright sun was bouncing off the water, searing the eyes of the unwary.

The other two Mexicans had swung inland. Flattened along their ponies' necks, they were riding hard and fast in an arc that would take them past the cottonwoods where the lawmen were sheltering, but at a distance. Wilde knew his son was right. One of those Mexicans would rein in when he was on the flank. The other would push on, eventually swinging round to take the lawmen from the rear. When both were in position, all four Mexicans would begin the attack.

'Gord,' Thornton Wilde said, 'I think you'd better begin making those shots count.'

'Both of you do that,' Lucas said. 'Coming straight at you, they're sitting ducks. Me, I'm a better shot, so let me handle those two riding across the line of fire.'

Despite the brave words, his movements were stiff and awkward. Face set, he bent to slip his rifle out of its boot. When he straightened, his brow was damp with sweat. His left shoulder was the problem. He could move the arm, could lift it, could even use it to steady the rifle's barrel — but each movement was agony. Angry at his own near helplessness, he shot a glance at his two companions, then bared his teeth and somehow got the rifle into his shoulder and worked a shell into the breech.

Wilde and Gord Bogan exchanged glances. Bogan shrugged, again faced front. Thornton Wilde joined him, and dropped to his knees. But even as he did so, he realized the situation had changed. While the three men had been talking, Wilde and Bogan briefly distracted, the two Mexicans coming at a leisurely pace along the banks of the Rio Grande had disappeared from view.

'Now where the hell have they got to?' Wilde said, frowning.

'Trees are thicker a hundred yards out,' Bogan said, flicking a glance behind him as Lucas Wilde's rifle cracked, then cracked again. 'I'd say one of 'em's in there.'

'One?'

'Yeah. The bank dips steeply in those hundred yards. Steep enough to hide a man.'

'Than that's where the second man's at — that what you're saying? They're working it so they come at us from four directions: front, rear, and both flanks?'

'One flank,' Lucas sang out. 'The feller on the left's out of it.'

Wilde grinned and looked over. 'What about the one hoping to take us from behind?'

'He made it. He's in position, and out of sight.'

Wilde sighed.

'Waiting never was my idea of a good time,' he said, 'and the older I get the less I like it. You boys set tight here. I'm going to give that Mex by the river the shock of his life.'

He stood up, straightened each stiff leg in turn. Then he propped his rifle against a slender tree trunk, drew his Colt and moved towards the edge of the trees. One backward glance told him that Gord Bogan was watching the front, Lucas the rear. Comfortable. Steady as rocks. Working as a team, each man with complete faith in his partner.

They don't need me, he thought. Two tough Texas Rangers — hell, if they hadn't been deferring to my age and judgement and Lucas was one hundred per cent fit they'd have picked all four of those boys off at a quarter mile and been away before the dead bodies came to rest.

As it is . . .

Bogan's assessment had been accurate. At the edge of the trees, the bank fell away towards the river. There was a steep slope of twenty feet or so, then a flat stretch of mud and gravel where the cool waters lapped.

Six-gun at the ready, Wilde stayed just inside the trees and began slowly to work his way downstream. He made ten yards, around a slight bend — and then he saw the Mexican. A fat, moustachioed man wearing a big sombrero, he was astride a bony mule, still and waiting. He was cradling what looked like a single-shot Sharps rifle. A big lump of iron hung at his waist — and that, Wilde realized with awe, was about the oldest firearm he'd seen in a long time. Colt Paterson, most likely. Probably rusty, but nevertheless powerful enough to blow a hole in the side of a cliff.

Suddenly, behind him, Lucas and Gord Bogan opened up with their rifles. At the same time, from the cotton-woods downstream and the position of the Mexican coming in from the rear, there came the crackle of returning fire.

That was the signal the fat Mexican by the river had been waiting for. Grinning, he shrugged his shoulders inside his loose cotton camisa and kneed his mule towards the slope.

OK, Wilde thought, let's see what you're made of.

He stepped out of the trees.

The Mexican saw him. His head jerked. The sombrero slipped to his broad shoulders, held by its neck-cord. Dark eyes glittered in the bright sun. Held in two big hands, the rifle whipped around, barrel gleaming.

'Stop right there,' Wilde shouted. 'Drop the rifle, get your hands high where I can see them.'

He might as well have tried to stop the mighty river from flowing.

The rifle barrel came all the way around. The muzzle spurted flame. Wilde felt the wind of the shot, brushing his cheek. As the Mexican flung the empty rifle from him and stabbed a hand for the pistol at his belt, Wilde lifted his six-gun. He fired once. The six-gun kicked against the heel of his hand. In the centre of the Mexican's chest, his shirt dimpled. The dimple had a black centre. Then the centre turned liquid and dark red as blood welled.

The mule was already making for the bank. Startled by the gunfire, it bounded forward. The Mexican fell, barely clearing the mule's slashing hoofs. He hit the dirt heavily and rolled onto his back. Wild eyed, the mule tried futilely to scrabble its way up the grassy bank. Then turned, slithered back down on stiff legs and stood shivering by the water.

Carefully, not trusting the man, Wilde slid down the bank and walked over to where the Mexican lay, arms outstretched, hands limply curled. He was alive — but only just. His breathing was wet and clogged. Blood filmed his lips. His eyes were already glazing.

Wilde dropped to one knee, reached out and loosened the sombrero's cord where it bit into the man's throat.

'Who sent you?'

The Mexican tried to speak, coughed, and blood dribbled onto his stubbled chin.

'Quickly. Make your peace. Tell me

who's responsible for this.'

The Mexican forced a grin, exposing glistening red teeth.

'Paco,' he whispered. 'Ees Paco behind eet. My good frien', Paco Ibañez — and now, you and your frien's, now you weel pay for what you have done.'

And then he died.

10

The remaining miles along the river to the border town of El Paso were covered at a comfortable canter and without incident. Gord Bogan and Thornton Wilde rode double on the Cedar Creek marshal's big sorrel. Bogan had, reluctantly, left his saddle behind, but hidden in the cottonwoods to be reclaimed when they had completed their investigation into the ambitions of Paco Ibañez.

Before they turned their backs on those cotton-woods, Wilde had insisted they bury the gunmen he and Lucas had shot. Gord Bogan was against the idea, and suggested tossing them into the river. The two Mexicans who had traded bullets with the Texas Rangers had fled, but there was always a chance, Bogan pointed out, that they would return with reinforcements. Get out fast, had been his advice. He was overruled, and the fat Mexican and his companion were safely put to rest.

The brief but violent fracas had breathed new life into Lucas Wilde and, while the fight lasted, it looked for all the world as if he had again slipped into his role of the violent Waco Kid. Or maybe not, Thornton thought with an inward smile. The boy was a Texas Ranger. He was formidable in his own right, and surely without the need of any assumed outlaw identity which in any case had been nothing more than a convenience.

Nevertheless, formidable or not, when they rode into El Paso in the late afternoon with the mountain shadows cooling the baked earth, Lucas was noticeably tiring. So much so that when they did locate a doctor — a bespectacled man called Merryman — and helped the wounded man off his horse and into the surgery, it was to be told that for the next twenty-four hours at the very least he was confined to bed.

And not in some dusty hotel room, the doctor informed them. The wounded Texas Ranger would stay there, where the sheets were crisp and clean, the air pure, and the young nurse dark and very pretty.

Which left Thornton Wilde and Gord Bogan out on the plank walk with time on their hands to puzzle over recent events, and their next moves.

* * *

'A Mexican called Paco Ibañez,' Thornton Wilde said. 'Does the name ring any bells?'

'Funeral bells,' said the man to whom the question had been directed. 'Lots of 'em, loud, clear and frequent enough to drive a man crazy.'

'Here? Across the border in Mexico? Or is he giving both the rurales and the Texas law the run-around?'

The other man was long and lean. He was stretched out behind a desk, ankles crossed, hands linked behind a head of thick grey hair. A badge was pinned to his vest. On the desk there was a hunk of timber. On the front of the wood, someone had used a hot iron to burn the words: TOM CRANE. MARSHAL.

'How long have you got?' Crane said. 'I could tell you tales from now until midnight. The man you're talking about's a cross-border menace, I'm running out of fingers and toes counting the incidents, and he's getting worse year by year.'

'Ahah.' Wilde nodded thoughtfully, looked across at Gord Bogan and winked. 'We weel have to be very careful when we catch up with thees *hombre*,' he said in an appalling imitation of the dead Mexican's accent. 'He ees — '

'Knock it off,' Crane said, grinning, 'and give me something to chew on. According to what you've told me so far, I'm looking at the Cedar Creek marshal way off his home patch, a Texas Ranger — '

'Not forgetting my partner, another Ranger not present but enjoying the hospitality of Doc Merryman,' Bogan said.

'Right.' Crane looked quizzically at Wilde. 'That makes for an impressive tally of law officers to be chasing one poor Mexican — even if he is a bloodthirsty son of a bitch. I can't check your qualifications, because the telegraph hasn't reached Cedar Creek. The rangers, on the other hand, have their headquarters in Austin and are just a wire away.' He looked at Bogan. 'If I send that wire, will ranger HQ vouch for you and your partner?'

'Definitely — though they might ask you what the hell we're doing this far west. But why waste time? You know we're not crooks, because crooks wouldn't be sitting talking to the town marshal. And crooks wouldn't be chasing — how did you describe him? — a poor, bloodthirsty Mexican.'

'Fair point.' Crane nodded. 'So tell me your interest in him, and if it sounds legal I'll see what I can do to help. Far as I know, Ibañez is nothing more than a small-time *bandido* who sets out on murderous raids when driven halfway *loco* by mescal. That makes him dangerous, but shouldn't give him the notoriety needed to attract the attention of Texas Rangers. But here you are, sitting in my office, so clearly I'm wrong and you're about to tell me why.'

It took Thornton Wilde ten seconds to tell an amazed Tom Crane that it had been suggested the poor but bloodthirsty Paco Ibañez was planning to reclaim Texas, another ten minutes to relate the story of a gang of outlaws led by another Mexican called Charlie Gomez robbing banks clear across Texas to finance Ibañez's dream only to see that money snatched from their grasp.

Mention of yet another lawman, this time a maverick, had Crane rolling his eyes in disbelief.

'So where is this gang now, these outlaws, Allman, Ryan and Jago? And what about the maverick lawman, Tindale?'

Wilde spread his hands. 'We were hoping you could tell us.'

Crane shook his head. 'Not a chance. El Paso's on the Mex border, so there's a lot of movement in both directions. And I'm like you, like any other town marshal: if a man's passing through and he causes no trouble in my town, I leave him alone.'

Wilde grunted agreement, but it was distractedly. His mind was racing as he thought over everything that had been said, the various happenings since he and Gord Bogan had ridden out of Cedar Creek, and his realization that to survive it was imperative he second guess outlaws playing a game he didn't fully understand. Hell, the truth was he didn't understand *any* of it.

'We were attacked, as you know,' he said, musing out loud. 'The only way those damn Mexicans could have known anything about us is from Allman and his gang. So both bunches met up on the trail, or outlaws and Mex *bandidos* came together here, in El Paso. If they're here, then so's Tindale, because he was ahead of them.'

'Unless they caught him,' Bogan said, 'in which case Marshal Tindale's already cashed in his chips.'

'That's possible,' Wilde said with a grim shake of the head.

'Maybe, maybe not,' Tom Crane said, unperturbed, 'but think about this. You downed two Mexicans, but two got away. After that short gunfight they most likely crossed the river, rode up the west bank and got here ahead of you. If that's so — and you're right about the outlaws' location — then you're in danger the moment you step outside this door.

'But here's something else, something you may not appreciate. I like your story. It's big, and by God it's got romance: poor Mex peasant claws his way out of the fields to raise an army and reclaim Texas. That's the stuff history's made of. It's big and I'm impressed — but I have to tell you, it's a load of bull. Ain't going to happen, and I'll bet my boots Paco Ibañez *knows* it won't happen. There's something else afoot, fellers, and, if you can stay alive, you'll find out I'm right. But . . . '

'But?' Thornton Wilde said.

'But you'll have to do it the hard way,' Crane said, 'because if this damn Mex's plan, racket, get-rich-quick scheme or whatever the hell it is, lives up to its promise — then it's way above my head.'

* * *

The sun had gone down behind the western mountains. Outside the marshal's office the plank walks were in deep shadow, the only illumination coming from oil lamps hanging from iron brackets that were spaced too far apart to be of much use. Pools of yellow light indicated their positions — but between those positions there were narrow alleyways and enough darkness to hide a dozen men holding sharp blades or drawn guns.

'We haven't eaten since I don't know when,' Thornton Wilde said, 'and I'm damned if I'm going to stand here dithering when my rumbling belly's telling everyone exactly where I'm at.'

'There's a café up the street, over on the other side,' Bogan said, teeth gleaming as he grinned in the darkness. 'The doc's surgery is round the corner. I also saw a livery barn not too far away and, if we're going after Señor Ibañez, I need a horse.'

'Let's go.'

Wilde stepped down into the dusty street and, with Bogan close behind, headed for the far plank walk. Out in the open, under the stars, he felt exposed but safe from a surprise attack. There were few people about anyway, most of the noise he could hear was coming from the saloon, and already he could smell the rich aroma of fried beef and onions. Or maybe that was his imagination.

So he was lost in thought, still trying to make up his mind on what he'd eat and how many cups of hot coffee he'd need to wash it down, when he stepped up onto the opposite plank walk — midway between two of the flickering oil lamps — and immediately grunted with shock as a heavy object came swinging out of the darkness and thudded with tremendous force against his skull.

11

They had stepped out of the nearby alley, two shadowy figures wielding clubs, lurking behind them two dim shapes bearing weapons with the sinister gleam of cold steel.

In that first assault, Wilde was saved only by the thickness of his Stetson and his attacker's wild haste. Nevertheless the blow was sickening. It slammed down on the still tender swelling raised by the butt of the outlaw Ryan's six-gun in the Cedar Creek jail. Muscles turning to water, the starlit night spinning nauseatingly around him, Wilde sank to one knee. Clamping his teeth against the urge to vomit, he ducked his head away from a second, vicious blow. The club slammed against a timber upright. The man cursed in Spanish. The club sprang back from the hard wood. Instantly the man turned that natural recoil into a clever backhand swing at Wilde's jaw. Wilde ducked. The club whipped off his Stetson, searing his scalp like red hot iron. He let his body go limp, flopped to the boards then rolled off the plank walk into the street.

He landed heavily on his back. As he shook his head he heard the thunder of boots, grunts of effort, the meaty smack of bone on flesh and knew Gord Bogan was locked in fierce combat.

Then his attacker jumped off the plank walk.

He leaped high and came down with bent legs, intending to stamp Wilde into the dust. As the man's boots touched his chest, Wilde rolled to his side. He felt high heels snag on his vest. The man's feet were plucked from under him. He fell sideways with a startled roar.

Wilde's desperate roll took his upper body under the plank walk. Dust rained down on him from between the boards. He was lying in filth. He spat, flattened his hands on the littered ground and twisted to look for his attacker. Like a cat, the man was springing to his feet. Feeling the strength flooding back into his body, Wilde used his hands as a pivot and swung both straight legs in a wide, scything sweep.

He aimed high. His boots slammed into the man's groin. His shriek was a high-pitched wail. He went down as if cut in two by a shotgun's blast, lay doubled up and groaning.

But what now? Wilde thought as he squirmed his way from under the plank walk. Two with clubs, two with cold steel of one kind or another. Those two held back because the plan must have been to kill the lawmen silently. That hadn't worked, so . . .

He came to his feet, rocking as he was hit by a wave of dizziness. For good measure he kicked the downed man in the head. The groans of agony snapped into silence.

Wilde stabbed a hand for his six-gun.

His holster was empty.

Scalp prickling, he looked towards the plank walk.

He was in time to see Gord Bogan grab a man's wrist and wrench the straight arm backwards against the timber upright. Bone snapped. The man screamed. A wooden club clattered to the boards.

'Behind you, Gord,' Wilde roared.

Bogan, the Texas Ranger, was well aware of the danger.

The man with the broken arm sagged against him, knees buckling. Bogan gripped him by his upper arms and held him limply upright, using his body as a shield. Even as he did so, a pistol cracked from the alley.

Temporarily blinded by the muzzle flash, Wilde heard the bullet thump into warm flesh. When next he looked, Bogan had released his now mortally wounded human shield. The dying man fell in a crumpled heap to the plank walk.

But now both the hidden backup men had emerged from the alley. The cold metal of their six-guns gleamed in the weak lamplight. Bogan backed away, half crouching as he went for his six-gun. In the street Wilde dropped to his knees, fumbling blindly for his unconscious attacker's six-gun as he watched the unfolding action on the plank walk.

He saw Bogan execute a clean, fast draw as the ambushers' six-guns spat flame. But the Texas Ranger was backing away. Wilde opened his mouth to yell a warning. He was too late. Bogan's heel rolled on the edge of the plank walk. As bullets whistled over his head, he fell backwards. One of his out-flung arms cracked against the timber upright. His six-gun flew from his hand. He crashed into the street.

That fall saved his life, was the thought that raced through Wilde's head — and in the same instant he discovered that the man he'd kicked senseless was not carrying a gun.

With a sense of impending disaster, Wilde stopped his fumbling and stood up. He saw Bogan climb painfully to his feet, stumble backwards, desperately shaking his head.

The two men from the alley walked to the edge of the plank walk. In the shadows cast by broad hat brims their dark eyes glittered. Both men lifted their smoking pistols.

Out in the street, the two unarmed lawmen were caught cold.

* * *

Four shots rang out in rapid succession. At the same time a door crashed open and light flooded the street.

'Quit that goddamn shooting,' a voice roared. It was the voice of town marshal Tom Crane. As his cry died away, there came the thud of racing footsteps as he ran across from his office.

At the same time, shadows fell across the plank walk higher up the street as bodies crowded into the saloon's open doorway and curious drinkers craned their necks to watch the action.

The action was over.

On the plank walk, the two gunmen were lying motionless alongside the dead man with the broken arm, their six-guns fallen from lifeless hands. Out in the street, Thorn Wilde and Gord Bogan were forlorn figures, isolated, unsure — halfway to being utterly bewildered, and feeling unutterably stupid.

It was Bogan who recovered first. He looked at the dead men. Swung around. Touched Thorn Wilde's shoulder, and nodded to tell him there was someone behind him.

When Wilde turned around, he was staring at his son.

'I got bored, so I slipped out when Merryman wasn't looking,' Lucas Wilde said, pale-faced. And then, as Tom Crane raced up, panting, he grinned and lifted the six-gun that had saved their lives.

'Lucky for you I did.'

* * *

The man whose job it was to remove the dead from the scene of gunfight or tragedy was a carpenter named Ben Driscoll who drove a ranch buckboard that also served as an undertaker's carriage. He was one of those who'd poked their heads out of the saloon. His curiosity had been mercenary: the town paid him a small fee when his services were required.

Always prepared, he had driven to the saloon in his buckboard. Ten minutes after the gunfire had faded into silence, the three dead men had been carted away to the town's funeral parlour, and the man who had attacked Thorn Wilde and would be walking awkwardly for the next week or so was locked in a cell.

For the lawmen passing through El Paso, and for Tom Crane, the night was far from over. Lucas Wilde had another tale to tell.

Keys jangled as Crane hung them on their peg in his office. Gord Bogan, at the marshal's bidding, was over at the stove pouring coffee into tin cups. Lucas was sitting down, stiffly, clearly in pain, but bright eyed and — in Thorn Wilde's opinion — too damn excited for a man recovering from a gunshot wound.

'I took a wander around when I walked out of the doc's,' Lucas said. 'I know Gord needs a horse, so the most natural place to go on the way down here was the livery barn.'

Crane hooked a haunch on the corner of desk, sipped his coffee, and nodded.

'Go on.'

'The hostler's an old man — '

'Will Craig,' Crane said.

' — and I could hear him snoring in his office. I guess he sleeps like the dead, because there'd been a whole lot going on he'd missed.'

'Like what?' Thornton Wilde said.

In reply, Lucas looked at Bogan.

'There's a grey horse in there, if you want it, Gord. No saddle-bags,' he said with a meaningful glance at his companions, 'but the man that horse belonged to sure has no more need for it.'

'And who would that be?' Crane said, looking mystified as he sensed the other men's immediate grasp of the situation.

'Marshal Reb Tindale, of San Angelo,' Lucas Wilde said. 'I walked into that livery barn and down the dark runway and he damn near kicked me in the teeth. Unintentionally, of course — that poor feller's hanging by his neck from one of those big overhead beams.'

12

Meg Morgan, the woman who owned the café, had been drawn from her bed by the crackle of gunfire and the subsequent squeak and rattle of Ben Driscoll's buckboard as he carted away first three, then a fourth body. Gord Bogan stayed behind chatting to her and Tom Crane when the Wildes walked up the street to stable their horses. When father and son returned it was to discover that the plump, cheerful café owner had been sweet-talked by the lean Texas Ranger and was about to open up and cook a meal for the three lawmen from out of town.

Tom Crane, after crossing the street to check on his prisoner and inform the dazed Mexican that he'd be questioned the next day, went home to his wife.

'What we've got to do in a hurry,' Thornton Wilde said, an hour later as he pushed away his empty plate and sat back with a sigh of satisfaction, 'is come up with a plan.'

'Before that,' Meg Morgan said, plump and flushed, 'what you do is promise to slam this door when you leave. There's coffee out back. The stove'll die out of its own accord, one of you fellows can blow out the lamps. Me, I'm off home.'

The door clicked behind her, shutting off their profuse thanks, and they listened to her feet thudding on the stairs at the side of the building that led to her living quarters. Another door banged.

'It'll need to be one *hell* of a plan,' Gord Bogan said into the silence that followed. 'We must've stumbled onto something big, because I've never had so many men try to plug me full of holes in one day.'

'No,' Thorn objected. 'It needs to be a plan, but a simple one, because there's just one objective.'

'Find Paco Ibañez,' Lucas said.

'Right. We locate him,' his father said,

'then we ask him what the hell's going on.'

Bogan grinned. 'Just like that?'

'Nothing like straight talking.'

'But there is the small matter of Allman, Ryan and Jago and Christ knows how many angry Mexicans.'

'So we get Ibañez on his own,' Thorn said.

'That explains what we'd like to do, but doesn't tell us how we go about it. How we do it constitutes the plan — and so far we haven't got one.'

'As Texas Rangers, we operate to our own rules, Pa,' Lucas said, winking at Bogan. 'That means without scruples. So tomorrow morning we talk to that Mex over there in the jail, and we force him to take us to his leader.'

'Force how?' Thorn said.

'You wait outside,' Lucas said. 'Then what method we use is up to us.'

'We'll see.'

'I guess that's a no. You don't approve.'

Wilde pursed his lips as he stared into his coffee.

'Crane would object to brutality in his jail. And tomorrow's a long way off. What I'm concerned with here is our understanding of what's going on. For example, this business of taking over Texas. The more I hear it mentioned, the more crazy it sounds.'

'I'm looking at the facts,' Gord Bogan said. 'One is we know Paco Ibañez is after a heap of cash. Two is, we know he's using Texan outlaws to do the dirty work. My guess is he's duping them; I don't believe in a Texas takeover. But I stick by what I said earlier: we're onto something big.'

'If it's not big this side of the border,' Lucas said, 'how about over there in Mexico? You think Ibañez is using American money to finance a poor Mexican's dream of immense riches?'

'What I think is, we won't know the truth until we talk direct to Ibañez.' Bogan grinned. 'But like your pa said, we'll begin pursuing that aim in the morning.'

'Right now, I'm more confused by

the minute,' Thornton Wilde said. 'I guess that's my age,' he said, draining his coffee. 'Let's get out of here and find something strong to drink before we bed down.'

* * *

It was after midnight. The saloonist behind the bar was a tall, dark man with bushy sideburns and slicked-back, oily black hair — a contrast in styles. He was standing back against the ranks of bottles, picking his teeth with a splinter of wood and stoically hiding his impatience as he waited for the lone drinker at the bar — a Mexican wearing a colourful sombrero and a blue serape around his shoulders — to drain his glass.

When the lawmen walked in he rolled his eyes, pulled out a battered turnip watch and squinted at the time.

'A half-hour, no more,' Thornton Wilde said to placate him, doffing his Stetson and letting his thinning grey hair inform the man that he should defer to age and wisdom. 'Flying bullets tend to dry a man's throat. A beer apiece should send us to our beds content.'

'If we had a bed,' Bogan said. 'You given that small problem any thought? I don't intend paying out for a hotel room, and I can't say I fancy sleeping in an empty cell.'

'I had a scout around when I spotted Tindale's horse in the livery barn,' Lucas said. 'There's a good loft, with plenty of straw. If you don't mind bedding down with rats for company . . . '

Silence settled over the saloon, broken only by the saloonist as he noisily poured beer into three glasses and set them before the newcomers. In almost the same movement he swept the empty glass from in front of the Mexican, then glared at him. The man shrugged expressively, cast a hard look in the direction of the lawmen then walked away shaking his head.

The door banged behind him hard enough to shake the building, an act of retaliation that caused the saloonist to smirk.

The three men at the bar sipped their warm beer, elbows on the worn timber bar, each involved in a spell of silent pondering. Thornton Wilde had no idea what the others were thinking, but he couldn't help feeling that Gord Bogan was right: they were on the edge of deep involvement in something big, but whatever it was it was not the takeover of the state of Texas. That story was a clear fabrication.

OK, Wilde thought, that story was being used to hide the truth, but there was no doubt that Gomez was using the outlaws, no reason to suppose he wasn't following orders given by Paco Ibañez. But if the Texas takeover story was a load of bull, why did they need to imagine something bigger was going on, something more complicated? Why not keep it simple? Like Crane had pointed out, it could be no more than a poor Mexican peasant called Paco Ibañez — aided by a couple of ruthless *compañeros* — using his wits and a bunch of gullible Texan outlaws to make himself a lot of money. What was wrong with that idea?

Well, just the one thing, he thought: Lucas and Gord Bogan were also following orders, and for the Texas Rangers to be involved it suggested something deeper than a Mex peasant and half-a-dozen bank robberies.

'What kind of dealings do you two have with the boys back in Austin?' Wilde said softly. 'The big boys at ranger HQ, are they always straight with you?'

'We're not privy to their innermost thoughts,' Lucas said, 'but that's OK because they tend to give us free rein.'

Thornton pulled a face. 'All that means is how you do the work is down to you. The Texas Rangers' prime role when they were first organized was fighting off the Comanche and the Apache.' He grinned at Lucas. 'The saying at the time was they 'ride like Mexicans, shoot like Tennesseans, and fight like the very devil'. I guess things are still the same, but nowadays they're frontier fighters, so they're combating lawlessness among raiding Native Americans — *and* Mexicans.

'Sure,' Lucas said. 'And as I've seen Gomez and the name Ibañez keeps popping up, the Mexican connection's there.' He frowned. 'So, what then, Pa? You reckon we're too gullible, taking everything fed to us by HQ in blind faith?'

'Not always. But this time — '

'All they told us was Texas money's going missing,' Gord Bogan cut in.

'Which was true,' Wilde said, 'but I think it's a long way short of the full story.'

Lucas was still frowning, absently rubbing his shoulder.

'We shouldn't be thinking too hard about Ibañez' objectives,' he said thoughtfully. 'Our objective's still the same: locate Allman, Ryan and Jago

— and Gomez. Those Texans have got the cash back off Tindale, Gomez is their link with Mexico.'

'Yeah, but is he?' Wilde said. 'As I recall, you were pounced on by Tindale because he seized his opportunity. You and Allman were left on your own when Gomez and the others slipped away for a meeting. That seems to put Gomez lower down the chain of command. It's possible they were meeting Ibañez — but my gut feeling tells me that's wrong.'

'Yeah, I agree,' Lucas said. 'Remember the talk that went on just before the jail break? Ryan and Jago were arguing? Jago was saying Gomez was the man in the middle and Allman jumped in, told him to shut up.'

'That's right,' Wilde said. 'And as there's never been any secret about Ibañez, that suggests Jago was about to let slip a name that's supposed to be kept secret.'

'Gives us something else to think about,' Bogan said, 'but doesn't change anything.'

'You're right,' Wilde said, 'so first thing in the morning, we start looking.' He cast a glance in Bogan's direction as he drained his glass and set it on the bar. 'And we take care. Mistakes made by one — or *every* one of us — have left us with one man nursing a bullet wound, and me with a head that feels like a tooth going bad from the inside. Not a record to be proud of, so we're going to look pretty damn foolish if they find us before we find them.'

13

A noise woke Thornton Wilde as the first light of day was filtering through the cracks in the roof over the livery barn's loft. Without opening his eyes he replayed in his mind the sounds that had disturbed him, and he knew at once that what he had heard was nothing more alarming than the rustle of straw. Close by. And as straw rustling in a livery barn, he figured, was about as unusual as a cockerel crowing at dawn, he opened one eye to squint at his companions then turned over to go back to sleep.

But he quickly discovered that disturbed sleep — for that day at least — was sleep gone for good. He lay there for perhaps fifteen minutes fighting the turmoil in his mind, then swore softly and kicked his way out of his blankets. He stood, stretched, yawned, slipped his feet into cold boots and realized that, in the semi-darkness, Lucas was doing the same.

The long bundle of tumbled blankets that was Gord Bogan stayed stubbornly still and silent.

'Leave him be,' Wilde said softly, as he buckled on his gun-belt. 'Let's you and me slip down and see to the horses. With them ready to go, we can make an early start.'

Lucas followed him to the open hatch, stood watching as his pa turned and started backwards down the creaking vertical wooden ladder with his hands gripping the worn rungs.

'An early start's no good if we don't know where we're going.'

'The first bit's the ride over to the jail to talk to that Mex,' Wilde said, stopping to look down as a rung cracked ominously. 'Waste of time, I guess; I can't see him talking, though Tom Crane being marshal of a border town may know ways of twisting his arm.'

He dropped the last two rungs, grunted as he landed heavily, then put a hand on the rickety timber ladder as he looked up and waited for Lucas to join him.

'If we do get nothing from the Mex,' he said, 'it'll be time to go looking for our friends the bank robbers — '

And then he broke off as for the second time that morning a sound screamed for his attention. This time not the benign rustle of straw, but the unmistakable metallic click of a weapon being cocked.

'Pa, behind you,' Lucas shouted.

Wilde was already turning, swivelling into a crouch as his hand reached for his gun. But it was too early in the day. His ageing joints, stiffened by a night's sleep, betrayed him and a stab of pain forced him down onto one knee. The fingers of his right hand fumbled awkwardly at the worn butt, turning a fast draw into a fight not to drop the gun. As he bit his lip in frustration he was aware of Lucas dropping like a cat from the ladder, felt his son's hand hard on his shoulder as the boy steadied himself before leaping desperately to one side.

Then all hell let loose.

The livery barn's big doors were open. Three men stood spaced out across that wide opening. The early morning light was behind them. Dark silhouettes with faces lost in shadow, they had begun walking forward, advancing down the runway.

And now their six-guns spat flame.

The noise was deafening. The gloom was turned to a bright midday by the blazing muzzle flashes. Hot lead screamed at Wilde from three directions. Bullets whined past his ears. Splinters flew from the vertical ladder. Dirt kicked up into his face from the hard-packed earth. Desperately he came off his knees and onto flat feet, flung himself sideways, wriggled like a snake and made it to the shelter of unopened grain sacks stacked against the wall.

He sat with his back against the

coarse hemp, gasping, the stink of cordite in his nostrils. He pulled out his six-gun, poked it out and cocked his wrist backwards to fire four blind shots. Then he pulled back. Reloaded the empty chambers. Looked across the barn, across the runway.

Lucas had made it to one of the empty stalls. Hidden from the outlaws, he crouched on the filthy straw and gave Wilde the thumbs up.

Wilde grinned. Now the attackers were out in the open and exposed, their targets under cover and out of sight. Abruptly, the guns went silent. In the sudden quiet disturbed only by the nervous snorting and stamping of horses and the ringing in his ears, Wilde listened for movement from the outlaws, heard nothing. He tried to put himself in the outlaws' place, and knew he'd do the same: wait out the opposition, let them make the first move. But he also knew that if he and Lucas did nothing, they were finished.

He looked across, raised his hand

with three fingers vertical, pointed to each one in turn. Lucas nodded his understanding. He grabbed the side of the stall with his left hand, held his six-gun cocked and tilted in his right, tensed so that he was a spring ready to uncoil.

Wilde did the same, though feeling more like a spring that was about to snap. Then he lifted his left hand so that Lucas could see it, brought it down once, twice — and a much faster third time.

As his arm whipped down for the third time, he leaped from behind the grain sacks. But as fast as he moved, Lucas was quicker. Across the way he was already out of the stall, a tall, slim figure standing with spread legs and a blazing six-gun in his fist.

Then Wilde began shooting. He saw the three figures, much closer now, and knew with a fierce exultation that they had been taken by surprise. Shock had given the two lawmen an advantage that could be measured in fractions of a second.

It was enough. And the closer they were, the better targets the outlaws made.

In what seemed like the blink of an eye, the startled outlaws began returning fire. But they were too late. Thornton Wilde was slow, but fired with deadly accuracy. Two of his bullets had torn into warm flesh. Lucas was also placing his shots with skill: two men were already sinking to the ground, their bullets flying harmlessly wide as the strength leaked from their muscles. Wilde heard one of those bullets punch through the overhead boards that were the loft's floor, and for an instant he thought of Gord Bogan lying in his blankets.

Just like me, he thought with amusement. *A sound will have disturbed his beauty sleep*.

Then he cleared his mind and snapped his gaze back to the scene in front of him.

One man was left. Gus Allman, Wilde thought, recognizing the lean shape and long hair — a man of a different calibre from his two companions whose blood was wetly staining the dark earth. One sweeping glance to left and right had told Allman that the game was up for Ryan and Jago. Without hesitation he spun away from the action. He ran hard for the wide doors. The street was a few yards ahead of him. Wilde had no doubt that the man's horse would be tethered within easy reach.

He screamed out a warning. 'Lucas, he's gettin' away, get after him — '

There was no need.

A figure appeared in the wide opening. In his hands he held a shotgun. The shotgun was cocked and levelled.

Allman saw it. He slid to a halt, took one swift appraising look at that shotgun, at the gaping black holes of its muzzles and the steady gaze of the man holding the deadly weapon — and he dropped his six-gun and backed off, lifting his hands in surrender.

'Keep 'em like that,' Gord Bogan

said, 'and you'll stay alive.'

He stepped forward, and kicked the six-gun beyond Allman's reach. Then he looked into the livery barn and grinned.

'I don't know,' he said, 'I leave you two alone for ten minutes, and when I get back you've started your own little war.'

* * *

'That's the way I feel,' Marshal Tom Crane said when Allman was safely locked in a cell. 'This may be a border town, with all the violence that goes with the territory, but I've seen more dead men in two days than I've seen all year.'

'And as it's pushing November,' Gord Bogan said, 'that's quite something.'

'Talking of quite something,' Thornton Wilde said, 'how the hell did you get out of those blankets without being seen — and where did you find the shotgun?'

'I walked out earlier when you and

Lucas were asleep,' Bogan said. 'You stirred when I made some noise getting up, but didn't see me. I went to talk to my pretty friend, Meg Morgan, tell her we might be needing an early breakfast. When the shooting ruined a promising conversation, she dipped down behind the counter and came up with this.'

He fondly patted the scattergun resting against his leg.

'Well, dead bodies don't worry me too much if they're bad guys,' Wilde said, glancing towards the door as Ben Driscoll's buckboard squeaked up the street carrying its latest gruesome cargo. 'What does bother me is the more men go down, the less chance we've got of getting to the bottom of what's going on.'

'This may be a good time to ask you to turn around and head for home, Pa. Like Tom says, you've got no authority here — certainly none if we cross the border into Mexico — and with bullets flying like rain in a high wind — '

'In a pig's ear I will,' Wilde said flatly.

'I'll unpin the tin, put it in my pocket and you can look on me as a hired gun.'

Lucas grinned across at Bogan and winked. 'Brains, yes, wisdom, yes — but after what I witnessed in the livery barn you'll never make gunslinger.'

'Brains might also be a problem,' Bogan said, deadpan. 'Did I tell you about the time I caught your pa crawling under his desk looking for that tin badge he's talking about — ?'

'Knock it off,' Wilde growled. 'I'm here to stay, so let's turn our attention to the man settin' in there looking at bars from the wrong side. He'll be feeling a mite lonely without his pards. Could be ready to do a deal.'

Tom Crane was stretched out behind his desk, a cigarette smoking between his fingers. He nodded thoughtfully.

'There's two of them out there, but you can forget the Mexican who clubbed you last night. He won't talk. Allman's a different kettle of fish. I gather he's the man took Tindale's saddle-bags and is now holding the cash.'

Wilde nodded. 'Unless he's already handed it over to Charlie Gomez.'

Crane shook his head. 'I doubt it. I took a good look into that man's eyes when I locked him up. He's smart. If he's as smart as I think he is, he'll not have been taken in by talk of a poor Mexican reclaiming Texas. And if he didn't believe that, then he was robbing banks for what he could make for himself.'

'The offer of some of that cash instead of a long spell in jail could see him switch sides,' Bogan said. 'He could begin by leading us to Gomez.'

Crane pursed his lips, looked at the glowing tip of his cigarette.

'Is that wise? Isn't it your job and mine to see he pays for his crimes?'

'Sure,' Wilde said, 'but you and I know he could have slipped across the border before we had a chance to get our hands on him. The fact is, he didn't. He's in our hands — perhaps more through luck than good judgement — so why not use him. Make the most of a bad situation.'

'My deputy did some asking around,' Crane said. 'The man called Gomez is well known in certain circles — though not to me. Seems one of his men was drinking in the saloon when you walked in last night.'

'Jesus,' Thornton Wilde said. 'That close — and I saw him and did nothing.'

'Oh, you did *something*, though it's unlikely to ease your mind. What you did was let him listen in to your conversation. Might be a good idea to go back over what you said, recall if there was anything of importance discussed.'

'Talked about sleeping arrangements,' Wilde said. 'I can't see a snoopy Mexican considering that important enough for Gomez's ears.'

For a moment there was silence as Wilde and the Texas Rangers brooded over their near miss. Then Wilde looked at Crane.

'What I haven't brought up so far is the possibility of another man here in El Paso — a man even Gomez has to report to. We got wind of this back in Cedar Creek when Ryan and Jago were arguing. Allman jumped in pretty quick to stop him when Jago was about to let a name slip.'

Crane frowned. 'But not Ibañez?'

'No. They've been quite happy talking freely about him and his big ideas.'

'So . . . any thoughts?'

'Well, you know we've all just about decided the Texas takeover is a cover to hide what's really going on. I'm beginning to wonder if Ibañez is really top dog — hell, I'm beginning to wonder if the man even exists.'

'Good point,' Lucas said. 'Those bank robbers did their talking around the camp-fire, and Ibañez came into it. But not once did I hear any one of them say they'd met him.'

'But if not Ibañez,' Gord Bogan said, 'then who the hell is he, and what's his game?'

'And if we do get to him,' Wilde said, 'will we have reached the top dog, or just stripped away another layer in a multi-layered plot?' He shook his head in disgust, then spread his hands. 'Well, if nothing else, we do have a contact. Let's go make friends with Gus Allman, see what that brings.'

Crane came up out of the chair and reached for the cell keys.

'A word of warning, Wilde. I told you this man Allman is smart. Take what he says with a pinch of salt, because at the first opportunity he'll work a double-cross. If you don't keep your eyes skinned and watch your back, your first visit to El Paso could be the last you'll ever make.'

14

To make any offers they made to Gus Allman more likely to be acceptable to a man looking at years in the penitentiary, Thornton Wilde asked for the prisoner to be released into their custody. That way, he pointed out, 'He'll be tasting freedom while knowing at any moment it could be snatched away from him. He'll also be comparing and remembering: one night in the El Paso cell will have reminded him of the years he's already spent inside, he'll be sniffing the fresh air while making comparisons with what he experienced then and what he's got now. Put bluntly, once on the outside a man will do everything in his power to stay there.'

So it came about that Gus Allman rode through yet another town with his wrists lashed to the saddle horn. His long grey hair was damp with perspiration leaking from his skin more from fear of the unknown than from the effects of the hot sun. Under his stained Stetson he was wearing a worried frown.

He'd not been told what was happening. This was a deliberate ploy designed to confuse and weaken the man and, as they rode out of El Paso and headed towards the river on the south side of town, it was clear to all three amused lawmen that Allman was fearing the worst.

Perplexity was written all over the outlaw's face. Had he finally gone too far? Had those in authority taken a long hard look at the procedure involved in arrest, trial and incarceration and said to hell with it, let's take the easy way out and get rid of him once and for all?

He didn't know, couldn't know. And when the lawmen turned the horses towards the green riverbank where waters lapped, called a halt under trees giving shelter from the blazing sun and removed his bonds, it was with a set face and nervously shifting gaze that the outlaw allowed himself to be led towards a tree and forced to sit on the grass with his back against a slender twisting trunk and his ankles lashed with rawhide.

'Strange way for a firing squad to act,' he said.

'Is that what you've been thinking?' Wilde laughed. 'Matter of fact you've got just two choices, Gus, and a firing squad's not one of them.'

'Three choices,' Lucas said. 'A man died in the San Angelo bank robbery. So, depending on how the judge and jury feel on the day of the trial, it'll be something like twenty years in the pen, or a stretched neck.'

'That's two,' Allman said, his face pale. 'What's the third?'

'You buy your way out,' Wilde said.

Allman shook his head. 'You think I've still got those saddle-bags?'

'Not buy with money, with information and assistance. Tell us what's going on, point us in the right direction. You were arrested by Reb Tindale. He was a crooked lawman, and he's paid for his folly. Ryan's dead. Jago's dead. Those last two deaths could be seen by the law as payment in full for the trail of bank robberies across Texas, especially as your involvement in those events is known to just a handful of men.' He paused, let possible implications of what he had said sink in, then said softly, 'Buy your freedom, Allman. Talk to us now, and you could ride away from here — '

'Your boy knows what's going on. We sat around a camp-fire, four of us. He wanted to know what he was getting into, and I told him: Paco Ibañez wants Texas back under Mexican rule.'

'That's a fairy-story. A man of your intelligence wouldn't swallow it, and neither did Lucas. I believe you know *exactly* what's going on, but you're persisting with that ridiculous idea because it effectively hides the truth.'

'No. I persist because that's what I've

been told. And that's all I've been told; that's all I know.'

'And you believe that load of bull?'

'Believing wasn't part of the deal. They told me they wanted cash. I wasn't concerned with why.'

Wilde cocked his head. 'So that was the start of it. Gomez offered a deal: you come up with the money for Ibañez, in return you'd get your cut — you, Ryan and Jago.'

'If you say so,' Allman said, shrugging his shoulders.

All three lawmen were sitting on the grass. They had formed a tight half-circle around the outlaw. Their six-guns were prominent. Wilde knew that with the tree at his back and the encroaching arc of menacing lawmen to his front, Allman would feel trapped. Instinctively, his mind would be searching for a way out.

Gord Bogan, hat tipped back, sitting cross-legged in dappled shade, was watching Allman closely.

He said, 'Didn't it occur to you they

chose that story of a Texas takeover because they knew men like you, men who'd too often seen the inside of hot, stinking cells, would be happy to see the Texas authorities in trouble?'

'If they believed that, they were wrong. Being in prison makes no difference. I'm proud to be a Texan; I'd fight to the death if Texas was threatened — '

'Then supposing it is. Supposing that story is true. We need you to help us to find out for sure, stop those crazy bastards, whoever they are. You keep talking about a mysterious 'they'. Keep saying 'they' did this, 'they' asked that. Who the hell are we talking about here, Allman?'

The outlaw shrugged, and gazed out towards the river with a thoughtful look in his eyes.

Wilde could see a noticeable relaxation in the man's posture. Quick to weigh up a situation, the outlaw would by now have worked out that if he could be seen to be co-operating

— even if he was telling another pack of lies — he could escape the pen, or the scaffold. He'd know that the information he gave and the names he named here by the Rio Grande could not be checked until he was long gone. And that thought gave Wilde a moment of silent amusement, because that wasn't the way it was planned.

'I can see you're coming around to our way of thinking,' he said, as Allman continued to sit in silence. 'Why wouldn't you? It's the sensible way out of a bad situation, and you owe men like Gomez and Ibañez no favours — especially now they've got their hands on the money.'

Allman shrugged, but said nothing.

'Have they?'

'They've got the saddle-bags, I've got my cut.'

'Your cut.'

Wilde hesitated, keeping his face impassive as he prepared to challenge the outlaw over the one glaring weakness in the Paco Ibañez story that hadn't yet been discussed. He looked at Allman, looked into the man's unreadable, colourless eyes, and shook his head.

'That's the bit I can't understand,' he said. 'Why take a cut? You and your pals were robbing the banks — why not take the lot, and to hell with the Mexicans?'

'Two reasons,' Allman said. 'First was that Gomez had connections. He made the raids possible because he knew the banks that would have money in sufficient quantities, and the date it would be there.'

'And the second?'

Allman jerked a thumb at Lucas.

'Your boy came along, but he was so all-fired keen to make himself accepted he might as well have been wearing hoss blinders. He saw Gomez. What he didn't see was Gomez's sidekicks. We agreed to take a cut because we had no choice. It was a closed deal: either we accepted, or we were dead meat and Gomez would move on and find others who would be happy to oblige.'

Wilde looked at his companions, saw Lucas spread his hands, Gord Bogan shrug. He took a breath.

'OK. So you were forced into it; you've done everything you agreed to do; you've been paid and now you've got nothing to lose by talking to us.'

'Only my life,' Allman said, his eyes narrowing as he stared at the glittering waters.

Lucas, silent up to now, gave vent to a rich chuckle.

'You scared of what the big man will do when he knows you've sold out?'

'Ibañez? I just told you, I was scared because I knew what he and his pals would do if we turned down the deal. If I sell out . . . ' Allman grimaced. 'If I sell out and he gets wind of it, I'm a dead man — but the only way he'll know is if you tell him.'

'You sure it's Ibañez? You sure he's not having his strings pulled by someone higher up?'

That puzzled Allman. He looked hard at Lucas.

'You know the answer to that: I know what I've been told.'

'That's what's worrying us. When a man's told something, the first thing he needs to do is separate the truth from the lies. That didn't concern you; all you were after was the money. But if you were concerned, I think you'd find Gomez has been lying to you from the outset.'

'Like you say,' Allman said with a thin smile, 'who the hell cares?'

'Texas Rangers,' Lucas said. 'If cross-border trouble's brewing, it's their job and their duty to care. And if you were telling the truth when you said you care for Texas — then you care.'

Allman shifted uneasily. 'Yeah, well, if you put it that way — '

'We want to put a stop to it,' Wilde said, stepping in quickly as he sensed a breakthrough. 'Gut feeling tells us Ibañez is no more than a name hiding a much bigger name who wants his identity kept secret. We need to get to

Ibañez. The link with Ibañez is Gomez. You must know how to find Gomez — '

'No.' Allman spoke flatly. 'Buy my way out, you said, talk to you now and I ride away — '

'I changed my mind. You help us — *then* you ride away.'

Gord Bogan grinned at Allman's discomfiture.

'Three choices,' he reminded him. 'I can't see you opting for either of the first two, so . . . '

'All right, all right,' Allman said fiercely. 'Talk of three choices is a laugh, because I've got *no* choice, so untie my goddamn legs and let's get this over and done with. But there's one condition.'

'You know the conditions,' Wilde said. 'Help us find Gomez, and you ride free.'

'If I ride away after helping you I want to stay clear of Crane and his jail. Crane's holding my Hawken rifle. I want it.'

Wilde shrugged. 'Consider it done.'

As Bogan took out his knife and did as Allman had bid, Thornton Wilde glanced at his son with a faint smile of satisfaction.

It was only when he was climbing onto his horse to lead the way back to El Paso that he realized Gus Allman had not been gazing thoughtfully at the deep, rolling waters, but at the river's far bank.

There, almost lost in the heat-haze, their heads sheltered from the baking sun by wide-brimmed *sombreros* and wearing light *serapes* that fell loosely to their thighs, two Mexicans on ragged ponies were sitting watching. They were distant figures, cloaked in anonymity, as still and as silent as the landscape.

About them there was a brooding menace that Wilde found impossible to shake off. It stayed with him all the way into town, a dark shadow dimming the small triumph of their negotiations with the outlaw.

15

All right, so he was locked in a cell again, a non-paying guest in the El Paso jail. Not exactly where he wanted to be, but there was a consolation: at long last it was a step in the right direction when, for the past couple of days, the simple plan that would bring him more money than he'd seen in his whole life seemed to be unravelling.

Allman lay back on the cornhusk mattress, watched the smoke from his cigarette drift lazily in the beam of late afternoon sunlight, and smiled with satisfaction at his lucky break.

His worst moment had come after he'd seen Ryan and Jago go down in a hail of bullets. Not because those born losers being drilled full of holes bothered him — them dying was part of the plan anyway, it just happened a little early — but because, when he turned around, that damn Texas Ranger, Gord Bogan, had got the drop on him. He'd appeared out of nowhere after Ryan and Jago had been gunned down by Cedar Creek's marshal, Wilde, and his boy, Lucas. Lucas Wilde, the Texas Ranger who'd stepped out of the dust of a San Angelo street and thought he was smart passing himself off as a gunslinger called the Waco Kid. Which, Allman was pleased to admit, had never got close to fooling him. OK, he'd argued for the kid against Ryan and Jago, but that had been a thinking man's choice: wasn't it better to have the kid on the inside where he could see him, keep an eye on him?

But it didn't work out that way, Allman reflected grimly. When he downed the kid with the big buff gun, they should have checked he was a goner. Instead, they'd let him sit there on that big horse and he'd lived to make himself a nuisance at the El Paso livery barn. One *hell* of a nuisance: Allman was forced to concede that when he'd been caught cold by the rangers the subsequent trip to jail had looked like the end of the road.

Then, damnit, the offer from Wilde had come out of the blue. Marshal Tom Crane had released him. He'd been taken downriver. And after a couple of hours spent arguing in the pleasant sunshine, he was back in business.

Arguing for the sake of it — though they didn't know that. Arguing to make it look good, to make it look as if those damn lawmen were twisting his arm. Just like he'd acted scared on the way downriver from the jail, acted like he didn't know what was going on, didn't know if he'd live or die. Hell, he'd known all along. They *needed* him, for Christ's sake, and he was *never* going to refuse what he was being offered, not when time was running out and there was so much at stake.

And time *was* running out, thanks to Tindale, the joker in the pack. Damn it, nobody had been expecting a maverick lawman to come out of the woodwork.

By taking them halfway back to San Angelo he'd wasted valuable time, put in jeopardy a plan that had been six months in the making and was just days away from execution.

Allman chuckled, his expelled breath sending smoke spiralling in the sunlight.

Aptly chosen word in the circumstances, he thought approvingly — both for circumstances in the past, and those still to come. Tindale's death had been an execution. And very soon, within — he took a quick squint at the direction of the sun's rays outside the cell's barred window — within, he reckoned, a little over twenty-four hours, well, there was going to be another.

Allman took a drag on his cigarette, his eyes narrowed.

What he couldn't understand was what the hell the rangers were playing at. If he was to believe what he was hearing, they had no idea what Paco Ibañez was up to. In fact, they were close to dismissing the man from their calculations and going after some mythical figure they'd conjured up out of their imagination.

But that was — what did they call it, academic? OK, *well*, it was academic, the *name* of the man they were after was irrelevant. The important point, the puzzling point, was they'd been alerted by the first of the bank robberies but they hadn't stopped him, and Ryan, and Jago. Known bank robbers — yet they'd let them run.

Why?

As far as Allman could see, there was only one answer: back at ranger HQ, someone in high office knew what was going on; knew what Ibañez was up to and had issued the order to back off and wait. That led to another thought: either Wilde and the two Texas Rangers were lying when they pleaded ignorance — or their HQ was keeping them in the dark. Giving them some information, but not all. A risky strategy, as demonstrated by what had happened as they followed the outlaws. Lucas Wilde, the Waco Kid, had been a plant, the man on the inside; he had come close to dying. After that, the lawmen had been left with no choice. They'd continued with the chase, nearly died in their encounter with the Mexicans set on them by Ibañez, and walked into an ambush in the El Paso livery barn. That one had been set up by Charlie Gomez, and again it had come close to succeeding. Would have done, too, Allman thought, if he hadn't been backed by two useless sidekicks.

So, yeah, a risky strategy, if that's what it was.

Well, the rangers had been right about Ryan and Jago, they had hated Texas for what it had done to them, and they had been in for the money. Allman grinned. Not that there'd ever been any chance of them getting their hot hands on any. They'd been recruited, and were expendable. Their job had been robbing banks, then getting rid of the rangers — and when that last bit didn't work out, well, at least he had the rangers themselves to thank for saving him a job. Tonight, Ryan and Jago would have been the first casualties, his way of clearing the field before the main action; before the six months drew to a close and he earned his money.

Not that he didn't have plenty already. And that was something else that was causing him considerable amusement. The lawmen were convinced the money from those bank robberies was taken to finance Paco Ibañez's crazy dreams. He'd gone along with the idea, managed to concoct an acceptable story when asked why he was satisfied with a cut. Truth was, the bank robberies came first, all on their own. They had been his idea, all the money was his (and, yeah, despite what he'd told the rangers, he still had those well packed saddle-bags), and it wasn't until some time after the first robbery that he'd been approached by Gomez. With a proposition. One that would double his money for the expense of a single bullet.

And as for there being coercion, Mexicans threatening to turn him into dead meat if he refused to do what they were asking — well, that too was garbage. They'd made the offer. He could have walked away. He didn't.

So, first things first, Allman thought, sitting up and using his heel to grind his cigarette into the dirt floor. By saving their own skins and getting rid of Ryan and Jago, the rangers had saved him one job but left him another. Getting rid of *them* was now down to him — and although they could have proved more difficult to eliminate than his two dead pals, without realizing it they were playing into his hands. Wilde, the ageing Cedar Creek marshal, had acted like a goddamn army general as he laid down precise rules of engagement: they would go after Ibañez when the sun had sunk below the western hills and the border town of El Paso was in darkness.

But they were underestimating the opposition, and that was a stupid mistake. They'd emerged from one gun battle with Mexican peasants with their skins intact, but common sense should have told them the men they'd downed could be replaced tenfold. That would have been done, because Ibañez always made damn sure he was well protected.

Also, Wilde and the two rangers were relative strangers to the border town. Its layout was unfamiliar to them, and by choosing to work in the dark they were handing him the advantage. He'd lead them in, the Mexicans would do the rest.

Yeah, it was real nice of the old feller, Allman thought — and, with a shake of his head at the way everything was falling into place, he lay back, closed his eyes, and prepared to doze away the few short hours to sundown.

16

'So what was he doing there?' Paco Ibañez said. 'Why was he one minute in a jail cell, the next on the banks of the Rio Bravo del Norte talking in a friendly manner to three lawmen?'

'I do not know why he was there, why he was free, nor why he is now back in jail,' Charlie Gomez said. 'But I do not agree that the talk was friendly. According to the men who were watching from the other side of the river, Allman was tied to his horse when he arrived; his ankles tied when he was allowed to dismount.'

The two men were in a small, thick-walled adobe dwelling on the outskirts of El Paso. There was no oil lamp. Instead, a candle flickered in the centre of a crude wooden table. Ibañez was smoking a thin cigar. Both men had a small glass in front of them containing the remains of a colourless spirit.

The room they occupied had one door, and one small window. Through that rough aperture the men could see a sprinkling of stars that were already being dimmed by the light of a full moon.

Unseen were the proud men they knew were out there, the small group of armed countrymen who had been crossing the border ever more frequently in the past few weeks. Six months ago, in the early days of the enterprise, there had been no need for them. Then word had leaked out of the suspicions and subsequent involvement of the Texas Rangers. Suddenly the enterprise was in jeopardy, and the man whose brainchild it was needed protection. In the past few days, as the rangers drew closer to El Paso, that protection had taken the form of aggressive defence. Now, in the final hours, Gomez had ordered the protective circle to be reduced and drawn in. A chosen few hardened fighters remained.

They formed an impregnable wall of steel around their leaders.

Inside the room, the two men were conversing in Spanish. The answer Gomez had given to his question had not satisfied Ibañez.

'If that is what those men observed, there on the river-bank, and they are accurate in reporting what they saw, what brought about the change? Why was Allman released, when you and I know that in the early hours of the morning he and his *amigos* ambushed the three lawmen?'

'The release was temporary. He is now back in jail. But his return was also observed. I have heard that he walked in without coercion. That his mood was relaxed.'

'Nevertheless a man in jail is under restraint. He cannot move freely. If Allman is a prisoner, he is of no use to us — and it is far too late to find a replacement.'

Gomez shrugged. He wore a faded red sombrero with a dirty fringe, a loose white shirt with baggy sleeves. The man in the saloon had been sent there by Gomez to keep his eyes and ears open. He had learned that the lawmen would be sleeping over the livery barn, and had reported back to Gomez. That the ambush Allman had arranged had come to naught was of no concern to Gomez. Two *gringos* were dead, but the man they were paying, the man who had been chosen above all because he favoured the Hawken mountain rifle, was still alive. And, despite appearances to the contrary, despite what Ibañez thought, Gomez was convinced Allman was a free man.

'I believe that he has been taken back to the jail, but not as a prisoner. I can only surmise,' he said softly, 'that they came to some arrangement — '

'That also might be a danger to us. Should we be concerned?'

Gomez shook his head. 'If I am right, it will be an arrangement that is no threat to our plans. Remember that Allman has always led a lawless life. I am of the opinion that his talk with the lawmen was about the bank robberies he was carrying out when I first spoke to him. The money from those robberies has not been recovered. Its whereabouts are unknown. It is possible that the discussion was about that money. Perhaps Allman was offered his freedom in exchange for its return, and is even now making final those negotiations.'

'You believe that?'

'It does not concern me. However, I am certain Allman is a free man. And I know he is mercenary. He has the money from his bank robberies and, despite his talks with the lawmen, he will certainly hang on to as much of that as he can, and I believe the money we have offered him will tie him to our cause.'

Ibañez nodded slowly, thoughtfully. He was a lean, balding man with a fine, flowing moustache. His shirt was a crisp white, his suit black, his leather boots highly polished. He drew on his cigarette, let smoke dribble from between his thin lips.

'You are probably right. Neverthe-less, I am concerned. There is, perhaps, too much activity of the wrong kind. Unusual activity attracts attention. Up to now the skirmishes have been distant. But it is important that nothing happens here to disturb, or unsettle — '

Gomez grimaced. 'If the rangers get too close, our men will be in an impossible situation. If silence is impera-tive, then gunfire is out of the question. I suggest — '

'I know what you are about to suggest, and I am ahead of you. Place the most hardened fighters in staggered positions along the route the rangers must take if they are to reach us. Order them to work with their knives.' He smiled grimly. 'They have Indian blood in them, those men, so they will like that very much. Sadly, the lawmen will not live to appreciate their enthusiasm.'

Gomez touched his glass, lifted it, then changed his mind. He was watching Ibañez closely.

'You think he . . . ' He let the words trail away, made a broad, sweeping gesture to indicate everywhere, yet nowhere in particular.

Ibañez smiled, again knowing exactly to whom and to what Gomez was referring.

'If he had found out that we are here, if he knew what was planned, he would have ensured . . . ' He shook his head. 'Let me amend that. If they had found out, those men he has employed to watch his back, they would have ensured that word never reached him, that Allman was . . . eliminated. Then *we* would have been removed. Silently. For what they believe would be the good of Mexico.' His dark eyes were amused. 'Silently, yes, of course: dead men do not make very much noise. But, fortunately for us, those men who watch over him are blind and deaf. They see nothing, hear nothing. They are fools.'

For a few moments the room was silent. A draught caused the candle flame to flicker. Gomez sipped his drink. Ibañez continued to smoke his cigar. At last, he sat back and sighed. It was a sigh of satisfaction.

'Tonight,' he said, 'it will be finished. Six months, from the inspiration to the culmination, the fruition of our plans. Yes, we have had some luck: for example, tonight there is a full moon. Allman is coming here — '

'Yes, he is, but there is one necessity that has perhaps been overlooked in the concern over his imprisonment. If he is to carry out the task for which he will be paid handsomely, he must know exactly where to go. As far as I know, he is unaware of the location.'

Ibañez waved a hand. 'Of course he is unaware; the location has always been kept a secret. But now the time has come, one of our best men must be there, outside the jail, waiting. But he must tread carefully. He must watch as Allman emerges, remain in the shadows if Allman has company; choose the right moment.' He smiled. 'That is the way it was planned, that is the way it will work, for the benefit of our country.'

Gomez nodded, basking in the glow the other man's words had generated.

'So, a good man will lead him and Allman will be here, close to midnight — '

' — and we know that conditions are in our favour. Allman will have a clear shot because the moon will illuminate the open areas between the houses, and because at that same time every night there is the solitary, leisurely walk from the cantina to the hotel — '

'Every night, yes,' Gomez said. 'A leisurely walk during which I am sure there will be a fast beating heart as the return to Mexico draws ever closer. But after tonight — no more. As his walk draws to a close, he crosses the small square on the edge of which his hotel is situated. His men, the men he knows are watching from the shadows, will not be able to save him. Thanks to Allman, his dream will be over, ours fulfilled.' He grinned, his teeth flashing white. 'And then, when the job is done?'

'When the job is done,' Ibañez said, 'then it is down to you, and when you have finished, Allman will be finished. There will be two bodies lying out there in the dust, and close to the bloody body of the Texan there will be the Hawken mountain rifle that fired the shot that will reverberate across our country, and across Texas.'

'Indeed,' Gomez said. 'Because of the plan we devised and executed with perfection, relations between the governments of Mexico and the State of Texas will be strained to breaking point.' He smiled. 'And, of considerable importance, we will have our money back.'

'If the Texan, Allman, has his saddle-bags with him in preparation for flight,' Ibañez said, 'we will have more than our money back. In just a couple of hours we will have caused political turmoil, and come out of it with a handsome profit.'

He reached across the table. In the guttering candlelight the two men were smugly triumphant as they clinked glasses.

17

Tom Crane had hurried home to his wife, with a promise to return before midnight. The prisoner in the jail was being looked after by one of Crane's deputies. With several hours to kill before they unlocked the cell door and got Gus Allman to lead them to Paco Ibañez, Thornton Wilde chose the saloon as the ideal place to pass the time. And he intended to spend that time in serious discussion with his colleagues.

'The problem is,' he said, as the three lawmen carried their drinks over to a table well away from the late-evening drinkers bellied-up to the bar, 'this whole business has got too damned tangled up for my liking.'

He sat down, took a long drink of cool beer with considerable relish, then set down his glass.

'We never did put much store in that story about Ibañez taking over Texas. The trouble is, we haven't come up with an alternative.'

Lucas looked puzzled. 'Do we need one?'

'Looked at from one angle, no, we don't,' Wilde said. 'We're going after Ibañez, and that way we'll eventually get to the truth. What I *don't* like is going fishing in the dark. If we're chasing the wrong man for the wrong reasons, we're certain to walk into the unexpected. Up to now the unexpected has been gritty Mexican peasants in big hats coming at us out of the sun with rifles blazing. Sooner or later our spell of good luck's going to run out.'

He looked enquiringly at Bogan. 'You sure your superiors didn't tell you more, give you at least a hint of what's going on when they sent you boys after Allman and his pals?'

Bogan shook his head. Lucas did the same and punctuated it with a shrug when his father cocked an eyebrow at him, and for the next few minutes the three men sat in silent thought.

It was Bogan he was looking to for a sudden spark of inspiration, Wilde reflected. The man had spent a year at Yale. That would have taught him how to organize his thinking. He'd have read books. Studied the history of the USA and —

'If it's not about Texas,' Gord Bogan said slowly, thoughtfully, 'then it's got to be about Mexico.'

Wilde grinned. 'You broke into my thoughts when I was just about to get there. Go on. Enlighten us. What about Mexico?'

'Remember what happened there, earlier this year?'

Bogan looked around the table, saw blank looks of incomprehension.

'OK, what happened was an unsuccessful revolt against Sebastían Lerdo de Tejada. He's President of Mexico. Took over when Benito Juárez died in 1871.'

'Yeah, I heard about him taking

power,' Lucas said. 'I was down in Laredo five years ago. Just a kid, but that's another border town and I couldn't miss all the gossip. I remember there was another Mexican whose name was getting mentioned a lot around that time. Man called Díaz.'

'Porfirio Díaz,' Bogan said, nodding. 'He was the man behind that revolt earlier this year. But he was active back in '71 when you were down in Laredo. At that time he was leading what turned out to be a futile protest against the re-election of Juarez.'

'So what are you suggesting?' Wilde said. 'That this cash Allman's been toting around is to finance a Mexican revolution? Paco Ibañez is going to try his luck where Díaz failed?'

'I was coming at it from another angle,' Bogan said. 'Like, maybe Ibañez is backing Díaz for a third try, and he's over here in Texas raising cash. But I know I'm wrong: the sums involved are too small.'

'Nevertheless, we've got two things

right, if we can believe Allman,' Lucas said. 'Ibañez is here in Texas, and Allman's given him saddle-bags stuffed with United States currency — '

He broke off. The saloonist they recognized from their earlier visit had been working his way towards them, flicking a dirty cloth across empty tables. Now he caught Wilde's eye and came over to stand close with the cloth draped over one shoulder.

'You position yourselves well for a secretive conversation, then spoil it by talking too loud,' he said in a matter of fact way. 'I couldn't help overhearing.'

'Where I come from it's called eavesdropping on a private conversation,' Wilde said. 'Usually warrants a boot up the backside.'

'A border town listens to both sides of the divide,' the saloonist said, unfazed. 'I can tell you now, if Ibañez is helping finance a revolution, Porfirio Díaz won't be the man leading it.'

'Really,' Wilde said, unimpressed. 'You got something to back that claim?'

‘Sure. When that revolt failed earlier this year, Díaz got out fast.’ He grinned. ‘For the past six months he’s been over here on US soil. I can’t see any reason why he’d want to return to Mexico to face a firing squad.’

* * *

They were back in Tom Crane’s office. Lucas had poked his head through the inner door and reported that Gus Allman was asleep. Crane hadn’t yet returned. His deputy, Ed, a stocky man with red hair, was sitting smothering a series of yawns in the marshal’s swivel chair.

Wilde was pacing the office, more than a little elated.

‘Remember what I said when we were talking to Allman by the river. I told him we saw Paco Ibañez as a name hiding a much bigger name. Hell, that saloonist has just about confirmed it. If Porfirio Díaz escaped to the US, then who’d bet against him being right here in El Paso?’

'Yeah, but we're still no closer to working things out,' Lucas objected. 'We now believe Ibañez is here as front man for Porfirio Díaz — but so what? Where does that take us? It doesn't tell us what they're up to, what their game is. You heard that saloonist. Díaz got out of Mexico, probably one step ahead of the *rurales* — and he's not likely to be going back.'

'I'm not so sure,' Wilde said. 'Violent uprisings are all in the day's work for political activists, Mexican fanatics. My guess is he's spending time here figuring out how to overthrow de Tejada's government. And I'm delighted, because we've finally got our teeth into a story that's fact, not a load of trumped up nonsense. We now know there's a man not a million miles from here who really did try to take over a country. We know he's linked to Ibañez — '

'No,' Bogan cut in, 'we don't know that.'

Wilde brushed the objection away with a sweep of the hand.

'It was your idea in the first place — '

'Yes, and I said I know I'm wrong because of the paltry sums of money involved. You don't overthrow a government with the proceeds from half-a-dozen bank robberies. Those small town establishments handle the cash from local businessmen and ranchers. We know how little that is: Allman's carrying most of what he stole in two saddle-bags.'

'Was. He's handed it over to Ibañez.'

'Yeah, and you can take that with a pinch of salt, Thorn.'

Wilde frowned. 'You don't believe him?'

'A Texas Ranger doesn't take anything at face value,' Bogan said, winking at a grinning Lucas Wilde. 'That's the way it should be and, as far as I can see, nothing here has changed. Allman's going to lead us to Paco Ibañez. He'll probably turn out to be some grubby Mexican chancer out to feather his own nest. We'll have wasted a lot of time doing work that could and should have been handled by the local law.'

Wilde rolled his eyes. Over at the desk, the deputy had begun snoring.

'If you're right, Gord, that would be a big let down,' Lucas said, suddenly sobering, 'but it's not what's bothering me. I was with Allman the last time he was in El Paso. We got nowhere, because Reb Tindale caught us cold and took us all the way back to Cedar Creek.'

'Meaning?' Thornton Wilde said.

'Meaning we got caught because Ryan, Jago and Gomez slipped away to talk to Ibañez. Allman and me, we knew who they were seeing but had no idea where they were heading: as far as I know, Allman has no idea where Ibañez is holed up.'

18

Although the moon was high, the narrow streets of El Paso in the areas through which Allman was leading them had pockets of shadow that disturbed Thornton Wilde. The four men were forced to ride in single file, Allman leading, followed by Wilde and Bogan with Lucas taking up the rear.

Too easy for Allman to slip away, should he choose to do so, Wilde thought. And too damned easy for him to lead them into a trap.

That possibility was rammed home when Bogan pushed his horse alongside Wilde's and told the Cedar Creek marshal in hushed tones that Allman was not leading, but being led.

'What the hell does that mean?' Wilde said.

'There was a Mex lurking in one of the doorways across the street when we left the jail. Allman was uneasy — remember I suggested he had no idea where Ibañez is located? I think he knew the general direction he was supposed to take, but no more than that. But he spotted that Mex almost straight off, and visibly relaxed. Probably been told there'd be a man out there — '

'How?'

'Note passed through the window of his cell, or a whispered message by the same route — but how it was done doesn't matter. The point is I reckon he'd been highly sceptical, maybe expecting a double-cross, or just to be abandoned and left to his fate. Anyway, he's been growing in confidence ever since he spotted that man in the shadows. I think the Mex is still out there, showing himself from time to time, popping up at intersections or bends so Allman knows which way to go.'

'If you're right,' Wilde said, 'then that scares the hell out of me.'

'Yeah,' Bogan said. 'D'you ever get that horrible feeling you're a lamb being led to the slaughter?'

He chuckled at his own grisly humour, and began to drop back. As he did so, Wilde softly repeated the order he had given when they left the jail.

'Remember, no gunplay. About all we've got is the element of surprise. Let's hold on to that. And pass the word back to Lucas.'

They rode on for a quarter-mile. The sound of their horses' hoofs echoed from buildings that were mostly single-storey adobe dwellings, some unlit, others with oil lamps visible through uncurtained windows. The streets were packed earth, filthy and uneven. They could smell dust, and the dankness of the river, the spicy aroma of Mexican cooking.

In the confines of the narrow streets, the ride seemed interminable. Just when Wilde realized impatience was making him fractious, there was a sudden commotion. It came from behind. He tightened the reins and leaned back in the saddle as he spun his horse. It collided with Bogan's grey, and for a few brief seconds there was confusion as the two horses tossed their heads and tried to swing one way, then the other.

Wilde cursed. He touched spurs to his sorrel and nudged past the confused grey. Thirty yards back, the moon was slanting through a gap between the buildings. Lucas was caught in the shaft of light. It was his muted cry of anger that had alerted Wilde. His horse was whinnying, tossing its head. A dark figure slipped out from beneath it. Cold steel glittered in the man's hand. Then, as the horse reared, Lucas slid sideways. He fell clear of the horse. The saddle was still between his legs. He hit the ground hard, legs flailing.

Out from under, straightening, the man with the knife coldly and brutally stabbed the big grey in the rump. Wild-eyed, the horse squealed and bolted.

Caught between amazement and disbelief, Wilde realized the Mexican had sneaked under the horse and slashed through the cinch. Boiling with anger, he drew his six-gun. Then, remembering that a single shot would ruin everything, he held his fire, slipped the weapon back into its holster and watched in frustration as the attacker slipped away down the street and was lost in the shadows.

Wilde turned to look for Allman.

Gord Bogan had pushed on for thirty yards or so, but had now stopped and was twisting in the saddle to watch the action. Beyond the big grey, the street was deserted. The outlaw was nowhere to be seen. Gritting his teeth, Wilde walked his horse to Lucas. The young Texas Ranger was climbing to his feet.

'I didn't see him,' he said hoarsely. 'First thing I knew, my horse was going crazy. Couldn't've shot that feller even if I'd been able, the bastard was in and out like an Injun.'

'Unless you can catch that horse,

you're out of this,' Wilde said. 'We can't ride double, can't waste time.'

Lucas was dusting himself off. His face was pale in the moonlight. He absently probed his injured shoulder with careful fingers, his eyes active as his mind tried to come to terms with the brutal act that had unseated him and injured his mount.

'He was a Mexican. You see what he did? He used that knife on my horse. It'll be losing blood — '

He grabbed Wilde's arm, pointed with the other.

In the patchy moonlight, Bogan's grey was dancing backwards. It moved as far as it could, then came up against an adobe wall. Even as Wilde swore and spurred his horse forward, Bogan's saddle slipped. The ranger went with it. He landed on his back. His feet were trapped in the stirrups. The saddle was between his legs. Another Mexican darted from under the grey. He kicked it with a booted foot. It snorted, and galloped away down the street. This time the Mexican didn't flee. He turned on Bogan. In his upraised arm, a knife glittered. He brought it down in a ferocious swing. Wilde saw Bogan belatedly lift an arm to parry the blow. He was too late. The knife thudded into his chest. Bogan flopped backwards and lay still.

To hell with silence, Wilde thought bitterly. He drew his six-gun as he reached Bogan and flung himself from the saddle. The Mexican was stepping backwards. His eyes were glittering. From ten feet, he threw the knife. It flew end over end, its whirling blade catching the light. The needle point snagged Wilde's sleeve, slid through. The sharp edge of the blade sliced his flesh. His arm was driven back by the sheer force of the thrown knife.

His six-gun fell from his hand. Clutching his arm, he stepped back awkwardly against the wall as the Mexican jumped over the motionless Texas Ranger and slipped into the nearest dark alley. Then Lucas came pounding up. He grabbed Wilde, looked anxiously into his father's eyes.

'I'm OK,' Wilde said. 'Nicked. No more than that. But Gord . . . ' He looked down, and shook his head as Lucas released him and went down on his knees alongside his partner. 'Jesus Christ,' Wilde said, sinking down the rough wall to rest on his haunches, 'what a bloody mess this is.'

Somewhere in distance, as if to emphasize the gulf between fulfilment and failure, a guitar tinkled a haunting melody of love and hope.

* * *

He was an old man, and he was alone.

Old? Sitting astride his horse on the edge of the moonlight, blood drying on his arm, up against the same adobe wall where his companion had fallen victim to the same knife-wielding Mexican, Wilde allowed himself a small, ironic grin. Too old for Oliver Shank's liking back in Cedar Creek, sure, so the town councillor had finagled his useless son into a position of power in the incumbent lawman's absence. Too old to find his own badge of office when the damn thing was snagged on his trouser cuff; too stiff to crawl out from under the desk where he was looking for it without banging his damn fool head.

Yet here he was, in the border town of El Paso, twice the age of his Texas Ranger companions, the only man left standing and with an impossible task ahead of him.

Find Charlie Gomez, who would tell him the whereabouts of Paco Ibañez, who would in his turn, perhaps, enlighten him on the aspirations and location of one Porfirio Díaz.

Fat chance, Wilde mused. Gus Allman had slipped away. Bloodthirsty Mexicans were prowling the dark alleys. He was one man on horseback, chasing shadows. A man on a mission that couldn't be explained, with no idea what success would bring — and to whom. Wilde shook his head, pondering. Gord Bogan was alive, smiling bravely through clenched teeth, but bleeding from a serious knife wound in the chest. A friendly Mexican had opened the door of his adobe to them. They had carried Bogan inside. The Mexican's wife and her daughter had begun tending the ranger's wounds with boiling water and strips torn from sheets. Lucas had gone with the Mexican to the nearby home of a doctor. *Out of my hands*, Wilde thought. *And now, so's Bogan's sacrifice is not in vain, I've got to see this through. Never mind the small problem of where the hell do I start. I start here, and I start now.*

He moved off. Staying in the shadows where possible, he took his horse at walking pace along the narrow, twisting streets. His aim was to find Gus Allman. Without Allman he was a blind man in a dark alley looking for the shadowy shapes of men he wouldn't recognize in the full glare of high noon. But the outlaw had seized his chance: the Mexicans had come out of the darkness with their knives, and Allman had slipped away. If he'd been telling the truth and had already taken his cut from the stolen money, then he would even now be putting distance between himself and the town of El Paso. Trouble was, Wilde thought, starting nervously as a dog slunk like an evil-smelling shadow beneath his mount's hoofs, he had a hunch Allman had been lying through his teeth from the moment Tindale walked him into the Cedar Creek jail. OK, lying was expected if a man was twisting the truth to gain his freedom. But when Allman had caught up with Tindale, hanged the hapless marshal from a beam and his share of the bank's cash was safe in his saddle-bags — when he was home and dry, according to him — then what did he do? Instead of taking the cash and getting the hell out of there, he'd risen at dawn and tried to gun down three lawmen in the town's livery barn.

Only reason he'd do that, Wilde thought bleakly, was for a heap more money. Only reason he'd be *paid* to do that was because something big was about to go down and the lawmen were in the way.

The street had widened. The moon was high and bright, shining on tiled roofs, on rusting tin roofs, on clothing hanging limp on lines stretched across back yards and on the clean white tower of a small church.

Baffled, with the feeling of running his brains ragged without making any progress, Wilde eased his sorrel into the shadows and drew rein. There he hesitated. Then, thinking to hell with it, he took out the makings and rolled a cigarette. The match flared. Smoke tickled his lungs as he inhaled, and he smothered a cough with the palm of his gloved hand.

'Something big,' Wilde repeated softly — and he narrowed his eyes as an idea stirred.

Funny, he thought — without a trace of humour — how one random thought triggers another.

Something big had sent his mind

racing in a dozen different directions all at the same time, and for some reason he'd ended up musing on the way Lucas had been shot by Allman using his big Hawken mountain rifle.

And then, with growing excitement, he recalled Allman, on the banks of the Rio Grande, stating the one non-negotiable condition for his co-operation. *Crane's holding my Hawken rifle*, Allman had said. *I want it*.

What had Lucas said, back in Tom Crane's office? 'We now believe Ibañez is here as front man for Porfirio Díaz,' and a few minutes later he had added, 'As far as I know, Allman has no idea where Ibañez is holed up.'

Supposing, Wilde thought as he drew on his cigarette, just supposing Lucas had been wrong both times? What if Allman knew precisely where Ibañez was holed up; and Ibañez, far from being Díaz's front man, was a dangerous enemy of the would-be president? What if Gomez was paying Allman to assassinate Paco Ibañez?

Fit the bill?

Damn right it would, Wilde thought, flicking his cigarette so that it sparked away into the darkness. And if a man with a Hawken rifle was planning on eliminating a powerful politician's enemy on a bright, moonlit night in El Paso, then he, Thornton Wilde, knew exactly where the killing would take place.

He was right, of course — but, frustratingly, he was also very wrong.

19

The way Wilde had it figured, a man planning on using a powerful rifle as an assassination tool would establish the time when he was going to pull the trigger, and he would set that time based on his knowledge of the target's movements. Those movements had to take in an open space: you don't use a Hawken rifle to kill a man in a back alley. With the time and the place settled, the assassin would then select a high vantage point that would give him a clear view of the open space. He would also make sure that after he'd fired the fatal shot, he could slip down from his vantage point and make his escape through the maze of narrow streets.

For high vantage point, Wilde thought, look no further than that pretty white church.

Certain that he was right, that Allman would already be up in the small, blocky tower with the bronze bell at his back and the big rifle's steel barrel propped on the stone parapet, Wilde knew it was time to abandon the big sorrel. He slid down from the saddle, tied the reins to a timber upright, then patted the horse and moved away.

He moved through the shadows, slipping silently from one alley to another, creeping stealthily past empty back yards as he avoided the open streets. As he worked his way towards the church he was using his long experience of life to come up with facts, and supplementing those facts with shrewd guesswork he knew would be pretty damn accurate. From his knowledge of small towns he *knew* the church would overlook a small square lined with a few shops, a cantina, and a hotel or boarding-house. What he was *guessing* was that Ibañez would spend some time drinking in the cantina, then walk back across the square to the hotel.

From high up, in bright moonlight, Wilde thought grimly, Allman couldn't miss.

Suddenly, ahead of him, the light began to change. The alley he was in twisted between the backs of the adobe dwellings. When he came out of that snaking turn he saw an opening ahead of him — the mouth of the alley. All such openings had led to yet more dark alleys. Now, ahead, where the walls ended, there was mostly light — and Wilde's pulse quickened as he realized he had almost reached the small square.

Carefully he eased his six-gun in the supple leather holster. He hugged the nearest wall. As he approached the opening, his eyes instinctively lifted to the white tower of the small church. It lay directly across the square, no more than forty yards away.

Near the top of the tower, cut into the walls, there were oblong windows. In the window overlooking the square, metal gleamed.

Wilde's skin prickled. He had got that far — but without a plan. The obvious action to take was to scream a warning when the target appeared and began walking across the square. But would that save his life? On hearing a shouted warning, Ibañez's first reaction would be to freeze. Confused, he would become a standing target.

The alternative was to begin blazing away at the window up in the church tower when Ibañez appeared and Allman was forced to step closer to the opening. That would do two things. If he, Wilde, was accurate — and over a distance of forty yards, with a six-gun, Wilde knew that couldn't be guaranteed — he would kill or wound Allman. But he would also send a clear warning to Ibañez, and when a man hears gunfire he doesn't freeze, he runs.

Wilde took a deep breath.

There was a third alternative — and it was the obvious one. If he began blazing away now, Ibañez would be safe. He would hear the gunfire from his seat in the cantina, and he would sit back, order another drink . . .

Face set, Wilde reached down and grasped the worn butt of his six-gun.

As he did so, an arm snaked around his neck. He could smell hot, foetid breath, heady spices. Muscles tightened, cutting off life-giving air. Then, in a deathly silence, he was lifted off his feet and flung back into the shadows.

* * *

'Gomez?' Wilde said, massaging his throat.

He was backed up against the wall. Several Mexicans with rifles stood around him. The man who had been choking the life out of him wore a sombrero that was a faded red, an embroidered vest over a white shirt. He still had a firm hold on Wilde's sleeve. He also held a wicked-looking knife. The edge of the blade was against Wilde's throat. Absently, Wilde wondered if it was the same blade that had been plunged into Gord Bogan's chest.

The lean man he had spoken to wore a black suit, polished boots. Under the suit his white shirt looked crisp. A black sombrero shaded his face, and a fine moustache drooped over thin lips. He was smiling.

'No,' he said quietly, 'I am not Gomez. And you will please keep very, very quiet if you value your life.'

As if to emphasize the advice the knife pressed against Wilde's throat. A drop of blood crawled on his skin.

'I am Gomez,' the man holding the knife said, and his eyes were as cold as wet black stones. 'But I do not want you to start a friendly conversation with me, because we are not friends, and that is not why we are here: to be friendly, or sociable — '

'I know,' Wilde cut in. 'Because very soon now a man is going to come out of the cantina and begin walking across the square. There's a man up in the church tower. He has a Hawken mountain rifle. You are paying him.

When the man begins walking across the square, the rifleman will kill him.'

'Is that right?' Gomez said. 'Tell me, why would he do that? And why would we *pay* him to do that?'

'Because there's another ambitious man, who is opposed to Sebastían Lerdo de Tejada, the Mexican President. This man failed in an attempt to overthrow your government, and came to Texas. Maybe he would like to take de Tejada's place, and be president himself — I don't know. But I believe the man who will soon be walking across the square is dangerous. He's the enemy of the ambitious man, the man who would be president. This dangerous man's name is Paco Ibañez. If you have your way,' Wilde said, 'Ibañez will die.'

One of the Mexicans encircling Wilde chuckled.

The man in the dark suit was no longer smiling.

'I am Paco Ibañez,' he said.

Wilde closed his eyes. He was leaning

back against the Mexican, held there by the encircling arm. In his mind he replayed what he had said, examined all his theories. When he opened his eyes again, everything had become clear.

'I got it wrong, didn't I?' he said wearily.

Ibañez shook his head. 'In a way, yes; in a way, no. I am Paco Ibañez and, yes, I am dangerous. And I am that ambitious man's enemy; I will do everything in my power to prevent him from becoming president of my country.' His smile returned. 'But, of course, where you got it wrong is that I am not the man who will soon walk across the square.'

'No,' Wilde said. 'That man has to be Porfirio Díaz.'

Ibañez nodded. 'Of course. And he is well protected. We are here, in the shadows. In other shadows, over there' — he waved his hand vaguely — 'there are other men whose task it is to protect Díaz. So there is a need for silence and' — the smile broadened — 'for Allman, the man with the big rifle who can shoot to kill from a distance and make fools of those bodyguards.'

Wilde stared at the neat Mexican. 'How much was it worth? How much are you paying Allman?'

Ibañez shrugged. 'It does not matter.'

'He's been paid?'

'*Si*. But the money will come back to us within the hour. Allman will gun down Porfirio Díaz and then he will die up there in the tower. Díaz's bodyguards will see to that. Enraged at what he has done, they will kill him.'

'That's the way we want it,' Gomez said into Wilde's ear. 'That's the way it was planned.'

Ibañez nodded. 'We allowed for it, planned for it. It is the finishing touch. Not only will Sebastían Lerdo de Tejada continue as President of Mexico, but a prominent politician — Diaz — will have been murdered by a Texan, on Texas soil. Mexican citizens everywhere will be very angry. There will be official protests from Mexico City. Texas will be forced to apologize — '

A man at the mouth of the alley lifted a hand in warning.

'*Preste atención*,' he called softly. 'Díaz is coming out.'

20

An evil-smelling hand came up and clamped over Wilde's mouth and nose. The knife was pressed cruelly against his throat. There was a low metallic clattering as the Mexicans with rifles stepped back against the walls. They blended with the shadows, became silent and still.

Ibañez moved to the mouth of the alley. He stood like a statue against the wall, not exposed, but not hiding. About him there was an air of expectancy; of inevitability.

Wilde reached up with his fingers and dragged Gomez's hand down from his nose. Breath hissed through his nostrils.

Against the hot palm he mumbled, 'Move the knife, I'm not going anywhere.'

Gomez's interest lay elsewhere. His

head was turned as he looked towards Ibañez, and beyond him to the moonlit square. Distracted, he let the bladed weapon drift away from Wilde's throat. Not far — not far enough. But now Wilde was restrained only by the hand clamped over his face, and no longer in immediate danger.

He was conscious of the seconds ticking away. There was no sound of footsteps, but he knew that Porfirio Díaz must be making his way across the square. He had been in the cantina. Comfortable, made drowsy by drink, he would be content to stroll in the moonlight. His men were there, hidden, but all around him. They would protect him. How could he possibly be in any danger?

Allman was high above them. He would see everything, but remain unseen. And he would wait. Then, when his target was directly in front of him, below him, he would pull the trigger. The big rifle would kick against his shoulder. The dying man would fall in the dust of the square, driven backwards and off his feet by the huge bullet.

Seconds, Wilde thought. *I've got a few seconds at most to save a man's life*.

He was thinking those thoughts, wondering how he was going to break away from Gomez without getting his throat cut, when all of Ibañez's plans blew up in his face.

* * *

'Let him go,' a voice roared.

Lucas.

Wilde twisted his head against Gomez's hand, saw Lucas several yards away down the alley with his six-gun levelled at the Mexicans.

As Gomez cursed foully in his ear and Ibañez swung around, his face contorted, Lucas pointed his six-gun at the night skies and fired three spaced shots.

'I said let him go.'

Gomez flung Wilde away from him. Out in the moonlit square, someone was shouting. Running footsteps could be heard. Gomez flashed a glance at Lucas. Then turned and ran clumsily for the mouth of the alley. He was drawing his six-gun. His intentions were clear.

'No, don't kill him,' Ibañez cried, and he grabbed Gomez, flung restraining arms around his body. 'Allman has no six-gun. For the Texan to be blamed, Díaz must die by the rifle.'

Then he stepped out into the moonlight. He stared up at the church tower. Like a priest about to bestow his blessing on an unseen crowd, he stretched up both arms and turned his palms to the night skies

'Allman,' he roared, 'earn your damn money, get on with — '

A six-gun cracked. His shrill, desperate cry was cut off. Ibañez stepped backwards. Then he slumped against the adobe wall and slid down to a sitting position. He sat in the shadow, dying slowly and with dignity; taking the knowledge that he had failed with him to the grave.

Lucas had reached Wilde.

'You OK, Pa?' He was looking at the blood on his father's neck, his eyes concerned.

'I'm OK,' Wilde said, shouting to make himself heard above the wild crack of six-guns and the roars of anger and pain. 'It's that lot out there who're in trouble.'

The Mexicans had forgotten Wilde, forgotten Lucas. Díaz's bodyguards had broken cover when Lucas's shots rang out. One of them had shot Ibañez when he stepped out of the alley. Others had shepherded Díaz away to a place of safety. Now all the Mexicans from both opposing factions were engaged in a bloody gun battle. Flashes lit up the night skies, bounced like summer lightning off the white adobe dwellings. Gunsmoke drifted in the moonlight. Bodies fell. The dust was stained with blood.

'If that's Allman up there,' Lucas said, 'what the hell's he doing hanging around?'

He was looking up at the church tower, and the dark opening where a rifle barrel glittered.

Wilde was wiping his bloody throat with his bandanna.

He said, 'You know, son, I think he went a long time ago. I think he went up there and placed his rifle where the moonlight would touch the barrel so everyone could see it — and then he turned around and got the hell out of there. You ask me, that man's many miles away and still riding hell for leather.'

'Took the money, and ran,' Lucas said, marvelling.

'Both lots, the banks' and the Mexicans',' Wilde said, as the firing began to die down and they turned away from the square. 'In the end, Gus Allman turned out to be way smarter than the whole damn lot of us.'

AUTHOR'S NOTE

Porfirio Díaz was a mestizo, born in Oaxaca, Mexico, of humble origin. He trained for the priesthood, but joined the army at the start of the war with the United States (1846–48). He served in the War of The Reform (1857–60), and the struggle against the French in 1861–67 when Maximilian became emperor.

After leaving the army, Díaz became dissatisfied with the administration of the president, Benito Juárez, and led a protest that was unsuccessful. When Juárez died, Díaz led an unsuccessful revolt against his successor, Sebastían Lerdo de Tejada.

That was in the spring of 1876. He then fled to the United States.

We know that Porfirio Díaz was in the United States. We do not know if he was in Texas, or in El Paso, and the events of this book are pure fiction.

However, we do know that Díaz returned to Mexico, and in November 1876 he defeated government forces at the Battle of Tecoac.

Porfirio Díaz was formally elected president of Mexico in May 1877.